All Aboard

Ragdoll Wife Leone

Matt Coolomon

Edited by S.H. Madonna

X-Rated

High level erotic content

D1523224

All Aboard: Ragdoll Wife Leone

Copyright © 2023 Matt Coolomon

Independently Published

ISBN: 9798377822608

Part 1: Braless for the Crew   3

Part 2: Leone Wants to go Topless   57

Part 3: Leone Gives Oral Relief   104

Part 4: Female Company for the Crew   149

Part 1: Braless for the Crew

Leonie

My husband leant around the doorway of our ensuite, shaving foam piled onto his palm. "He didn't actually say that though?"

"Well no, not in so many words of course."

"But he implied it – that if you go to this thing with him he'll let us have the new sonar?"

"Um no, let me see…" I thought back to what my boss, the Vice Chancellor of the university, had offered me exactly. "I think his words were that if I 'accompanied him over the weekend' he'd see to it that our application was 'looked at again, perhaps more favourably', I think is how he put it. But only because of how much he needs my 'note-taking skills'. There's going to be wall-to-wall lectures and he can't take notes to save his life."

"Right." My husband leant back again, face foamed-up, razor in hand. God he smells good when he's shaving. "So your note-taking skills huh? And he's never heard of recording?"

I bit my lip and smiled. "He doesn't want to attend in person, is his problem." I was losing interest in talking about my boss real fast.

I was still in bed. I pushed my pyjama shorts down and took them off.

My husband *looks* good when shaving too. He was in his trousers and shoes but only a white singlet top. He has a nice lithe build, strong broad shoulders. He was still going on about the fact that our research funding application had been refused by the university. I felt between my legs. I was already moist and became more slick as I played with my clit.

"Um, Clark?" I asked sweetly.

He had rinsed and was dabbing his face with a fluffy white towel. He looked around the doorway again. I was smiling and biting my lip. He frowned after glancing at my pyjama bottoms on the floor. He checked his watch. "I'm going to be late, baby."

I lifted my chin. "Just one kiss?"

He chuckled and rolled his eyes as he approached.

He met my lips. He smelt so damn good. He had the towel slung around his neck. I grabbed and gathered it in one hand, pulling down on it as I kicked the bed clothes back.

"Aw hell Leonie, seriously? Right now?"

I glared at him. He knows he's not allowed to speak.

I kept hold of the towel around his neck and pushed the top of his head down. He submitted and lowered to his knees on the floor. I forced his head between my legs, spinning sideways on the edge of the bed, resting my feet on my obedient husband's shoulders. "Uh huh," I told him as he licked where I'd already opened my pussy lips and exposed my slick inner folds.

My husband licked and nuzzled into me, sucking gently on my labia and teasing my swollen little button. He added his fingers and inserted to massage back against my pubic bone and growled into my pussy while I pulled on his hair and pressed myself on his smoothly shaven face.

Mmm this never takes long in the morning. I'd woken up horny, having had some lovely dreams then being turned on more with Clark's deodorant and shaving cream aroma. "Mmuh huh huh," I moaned, shuddering as my orgasm clenched and thumped through my body. I kept hold of his hair and let the waves of pleasure wash through me for a moment. "Mmm thank you, husband," I hummed and pushed him away to spin back around into bed and pull the covers up.

He stood wiping his face with his hands. I giggled. I know he likes wearing my juices to work.

"Run along now, don't be late," I told him, glancing down at his boner in his pants and back up again to giggle some more.

He bent and kissed me on the lips. "You just fucking wait," he warned.

I giggled some more after tasting myself on my now sticky lips.

Clark pulled on his shirt and hurried for the door to catch his bus. I hoped he wouldn't miss it again, but I seriously needed that little bit of seeing to this morning. Especially after what we'd been talking about. There was no way on earth I'd ever 'accompany' my fat sleazy boss anywhere, but I was so turned on by the idea of being coerced into sex.

Clark and I had met at a BDSM exhibition, both of us there out of curiosity and intrigued by the idea of submission and control. We're a little bit kinky, as far as young married people go I think. We don't talk about anything of the sort with our friends or family. *God no!*

No, we're closet kinky and only ever do stuff in the privacy of our marital bedroom. And there was seriously not a hope in hell I'd even look at my boss in that way. But it was still exciting to be illegally hit on by him, sexually harassed in my workplace no less, although he was very good at not technically saying anything. He just ogles a lot but never touches.

I kicked off the bed clothes again, sat up and looked at my suitcases in the corner of the room. I was all packed and ready. Tomorrow morning we were going to be a full four weeks at sea and I couldn't wait. I'm a bit of a water baby and have always been drawn to the ocean.

Clark was a Research Fellow in Modern History at university, I was Executive Assistant to the Vice

Chancellor, a Professor of Modern History. Clark and his team had recently returned from salvaging artefacts from a 250-year-old French shipwreck near one of the remote South Pacific islands. He decided we should spend our holiday going back to look for a British shipwreck Clark believed was on the other side of the island.

It was going to take nine days to sail there so we had chartered a yacht with two crew for 28 days. Clark believed he knew the near exact co-ordinates. A recent nearby volcano and subsequent tsunami could potentially have shifted enough sediment to uncover the vessel like it had done for the other shipwreck. And if the ocean currents were favourable, the shipwreck may well have revealed itself and its long-hidden secrets. There were journal entries in the manifest of explorers from a century ago that detailed the wreck having been uncovered after a severe storm back then.

This whole shipwreck thing was part of Clark's research for his PHD. I was more interested in the cruise itself, as we were going on a beautiful yacht and the crew were really nice. I'd been on a weekend sail last summer to a wreck just off the coast. It was going to be so fantastic sailing all the way around the northern tip of New Zealand and up into the tropics. I could not wait.

Clark

The last day before our annual vacation was busy of course. I gave a lecture in the morning to a packed theatre and was held up afterward by a few students who don't read their assignment instructions properly.

I got away fifteen minutes late and only just caught my charter boat captain, Dick Dastardly, well Dirk actually – looks like he'd just about given up waiting for me on the jetty and had started to head to the local bar for his lunch when he spotted me.

"Yeah, I've only got a few minutes myself... Skylark's good to go though," he said motioning towards the yacht. "We're all fuelled up. Just need to finish stocking the galley this afternoon and we're all set to sail at 9am."

"Okay, excellent. Are Linus and Victoria here?" I was being ushered aboard.

The yacht was a sleek-lined 18 metre vessel 90% owned by a wealthy businessman and his wife, who were going to be joining us for the voyage, strictly as tourists they had enthused.

"Nah man, Linus had some business to finish up this morning. Said he'd see you both tonight at dinner. How about um... ah here she is now!" Dirk's face split into a huge smile as my lovely wife approached along the jetty. "This is Santos, by the way. My new deckhand."

A young slim dark-skinned guy had appeared from below deck and his eyes widened too as he spotted Leonie waving at us and smiling broadly herself.

My wife always does this. Away from work she never bothers with a bra, and her smallish highset nipples are eternally erect and prominent through her tops. She's only a B-cup but her tits tend to jiggle a lot as she walks too. It's quite the show and has every man's eyes popping out of their sockets without fail.

"Hi Dirk! How are you?" she sang gaily as she walked up the gangway and right into his arms.

Dirk is tall and rather well built. His long arms reached all the way around Leonie and I noticed one hand had wrapped under her tit with the thumb pointing upwards, pressing firmly into it.

I was going to have to get used to this again. Leonie is way too friendly and this guy takes advantage. But his was the only charter fee anywhere near my budget. And with the owners tagging along I'd only be paying a fraction of the fuel costs.

"Come on and have a look then." Dirk had refurbished the cabin and was keen to show us. He still had hold of my wife, one arm around her and guiding her to the stairs.

Leonie claimed his arm and plied his hand from her person but she kept hold of it. He followed right behind her. I tagged along down into the galley and lounge area. There was one single berth and the one double. There were two spacious lounge areas, one on this level and one upstairs on the top deck. The boat had three levels all up. The bridge was luxuriously appointed with another small sleeping berth, extra food and equipment storage and bathroom facilities.

The last time Leonie and I had spent time on Dirk's yacht was a fun weekend away to explore a wreck less than a day's sailing from the marina. It was just the three of us. We had taken the runabout across to a small, completely secluded beach with pristine water where I had allowed Dirk to talk us into Leonie go topless.

He had talked us both around. *Yes, quite the smooth talker...*

I was excited to see if Leonie would actually do it. She was a little reluctant but had finally taken off her bikini top for several hours whilst sunbathing and swimming.

So the guy had already seen her tits once!

Leonie led the way through the boat, excitedly checking it all out. Dirk's eyes zeroed in and his hands often brushed or squeezed rather close to her jiggling little globes and pebble-hard button nipples.

We were up on the top deck now, checking out the refurbished barbeque and outdoor kitchen, dining area. I met my wife's grimace as I looked up from Dirk's huge hand squeezing just beneath her boob again, her clinging to his wrist at her side. She knew what I was thinking and

I'm sure she was thinking the same thing herself – that this was exactly what we thought was going to happen. We knew we'd have to learn to put up with it if we wanted to go find the wreck of the legendary HMS Sunline, lost off the South Pacific Island of Mahacu in 1792, purportedly carrying an off-manifest war bounty of treasures.

Leonie

The work done in refurbishing the yacht was amazing. It was great before, although obviously looking a little tired. But now all the timber work was polished like new and all leather and cloth furniture coverings had been replaced. The double bedroom looked beautiful and was going to be so nice for us girls to stay in. The sleeping arrangements were for us ladies to share the double berth and for the gentlemen to make do with wherever they could get comfy. There were only four of them and plenty of room with the other single berth, which would probably be claimed by Linus. There were ample choices of indoor and outdoor lounges for Clark, Dirk and Santos to haggle over.

The only issue was going to be privacy. It was only a small cruiser, no super-yacht that's for sure. But we could all make do for a few weeks. I was more than happy to share with Victoria. We had a queen-size bed and were both only small. We won't even know the other's in the bed.

I liked the new deckhand, Santos. He seemed a nice boy, very polite with a great smile. I'd felt his eyes on me a bit, but that's typical of guys and I was fine with it. I don't see why I should wear a bra when I don't really need to. It would only be a modesty thing to reduce a bit of movement and stop my nipples from showing so obviously, but what the hell right? Girls have boobs. So what! And if guys can't help ogling then I take that as a compliment.

Hell, it makes them smile not frown, so it must be a good thing in my book. Who doesn't like making people smile?

I have a range of t-shirts, tanks and tube tops. They all hug tight and some of the lighter coloured ones, like the blue tank I was wearing today, showed a bit more than the position of my nipples. Which are bullets with a small areola, quite dark. The guys could see them quite well, but I knew that and had chosen the top on purpose today.

I have five light coloured tops that are purposely thin and more see-through than others. I often wear one of them when we go to the beach or somewhere for a weekend drive where we won't bump into anyone we know. Depending on the reaction I got from Victoria, I intended to rotate between the five all the while onboard the yacht.

I wanted to do it for Dirk and his young deckhand, now it was obvious he liked it. But mostly it was going to be for my husband. It makes him so competitive for me and so forceful in the bedroom. I love that.

Every time I wear one of my thin stretchy tops and show more nipple, he ravishes me that night. I first noticed it by accident, when I only had the one pale yellow top that showed too much. I hadn't bought that on purpose, it was just really old and had worn and faded. But noticing how much my husband clearly enjoyed it, I bought another. Then another three. Then I tossed away the faded old yellow one.

I was also hoping for an opportunity to go fully topless again on this trip. Again it depended on this older couple, and how they'd feel about me doing that, or whether there would be a chance at the island if they were not around at some point. It was obvious that Dirk would want me to again, and I doubted Santos would complain. It was too bad Linus and Victoria weren't there today as I'd been hoping to gauge their reaction to my see-through tank top before we headed out to sea.

Well anyway, not to worry. I saw the look in my husband's eyes and I knew I was going to be in trouble tonight haha.

I had just dropped Clark at his lecture theatre and I needed to grab my iPad from my desk drawer. I hoped I had left it there at least. I couldn't find it anywhere at home this morning and absolutely needed it for reading on the trip. Oh my god how would I survive all those ocean hours day after day without my eBooks!

I snuck into the admin building via a back door, a bit self-conscious about my skimpy attire and hoping not to bump into my sleazy boss. I said a quick hello and got some looks from a few of my colleagues but kept my arms folded as much as I could. Vice Chancellor Hugo was busy on his phone with his chair turned around. I snuck past his office window unseen and luckily found my iPad in my desk drawer.

"Leonie! Aren't you supposed to be on vacation?"

"Oh hi Professor Norris."

Oh my god I was blushing now. This was even worse than the VC. His golden boy!

"So um… you're not seriously still planning that expedition, are you Leonie?" He slipped onto the edge of my desk, trapping my escape route. "I see they didn't approve Clark's request for the new sonar. Even if there was a wreck around that southern side of the headland, there'd be no chance of finding it with a searchlight system, he'd need the ultrasonic and this new software."

"Well, I'm sure Clark knows what he's doing, Professor Norris. And no we haven't given up on our expedition at all. We're sailing tomorrow as a matter of fact."

The man smiled. Damn it! He had a gorgeous smile. Smelt good too. I didn't know what had gotten into me, the way men smelt today. Dirk had been sweaty and unfresh but that had made me all giddy and had me smiling my head off too.

Professor Norris was going on about his progress extracting artefacts from the French wreck. He was in charge of that, as a Senior Research Fellow in the Modern History faculty. Technically my husband's boss, unfortunately. Although Clark was taking annual leave too, so he wasn't answerable to the university.

"Well yes, I suppose ours is in fact a treasure hunt," I agreed. "And why not, how cool would it be to find a sunken treasure!"

Professor Norris laughed with me, not at me. He was an arrogant dick but had a pleasant side too. I'd inadvertently relaxed from keeping my arms folded and his eyes were on my boobs quite regularly. *That's definitely working haha...*

"So, you all finished out there now?" I asked. "Why didn't the university let Clark use the upgraded sonar and software?"

The man shrugged. "Not sure. You'd have to ask the VC," he skilfully evaded and had an overt look down and up from my boobs this time. "But yeah, we're still salvaging, another few weeks yet." He had another look at where I had my arms folded tight again. "Might even see you out there hey, Leonie?"

I held his stare and edged past between the wall and his knee. I virtually had to straddle his knee to get by. "Not sure. You'd have to speak to my husband about that," I tossed over my shoulder in exactly the same skilfully evasive tone he'd used on me a moment ago. And I glanced back on my way down the stairs to see him still smiling after me, giving a little one finger salute.

The problem with Professor Norris for me, like with Dirk, is that he's built so powerfully. I love my husband's lithe build and broad shoulders. These other men are both older, in their mid-thirties, so more mature and kind of rugged looking. And they both obviously work out. Their arms are huge and their shoulders are not just broad but bulging with muscles that fill their t-shirts and ripple down their backs. They both have large muscular thighs and tight-looking little butts.

Oh stop it Leonie!

I had to stop thinking like this. I didn't want to be prematurely wet for my husband tonight and spoil all his fun. I went home and put on a different top to go visit my mother. She had a couple of bottles of full block-out sunscreen for me, always worrying about my skin and encouraging me to use extra strength lotion. I didn't dare tell her I wanted to try tanning my boobs. Although she used to be a hippie chick back in her day and was probably more risqué than I could ever be.

I dressed conservatively for our dinner with Linus and Victoria that night. I had met them once before but didn't know what to expect in a social setting. They were fun actually. Linus turned out to be a bit of a clown, always making a joke out of everything, and Victoria got very happy after two glasses of wine.

"Oh this is going to be our girls' Pacific cruise, isn't it sweetie! These boys are only coming along as our wait staff and boat drivers or whatever they have to do. Clark here can be our navigator and Linus loves to cook. Those other two boys can steer the boat and have turns running after us."

"Oh I agree. Definitely a girls' cruise," I said hugging Victoria's arm within mine and glaring playfully at the men sitting opposite. "Can you really cook, Linus?"

"Yes it's my thing, I suppose."

"Oh Linus is an old restaurateur from way back, aren't you Smokey? Wait till you taste what he can do on one of these barbeques!"

It came to light in further conversation that Linus was a trained chef but made his money in bar and grill dining, where we were right now at the marina, at a bar and grill. Turns out they owned it.

I'd been wondering about the fantastic service we'd been getting. My steak and prawns were delicious too. Those and the two bottles of red I helped my new older girlfriend put away before we left them looking forward to

21

meeting on the yacht in the morning and getting an Uber home.

It was quite late. We were packed ready to sail. I showered and waited in bed for Clark to finish up some online university work. I noticed his bottle of lube on the sink in the ensuite, so I knew I was in for it. I tried to put that out of my mind and remain calm.

He finally turned off the lights out in the kitchen and living room and came into the bedroom. I lay on my side facing away from the ensuite, my legs bent up, just in a nightie and no panties with a sheet pulled over me. I caught a breath as Clark lifted the bed clothes, folding them over me and exposing my butt. I clutched the sheet in two hands under my chin and waited while he went and washed his face and brushed his teeth.

The tap turned off. I heard the lid of the lubricant bottle pop open.

I measured my breaths. My butt was cold from being exposed, although it was a warm enough evening. I heard the oily squish of my husband lubricating himself. I felt the

22

weight of him kneeling on the bed. Then I felt him touch my pussy, probing, poking, then he slid into me.

"Uhh hhh huh," I moaned but bit down hard to suppress any sound as my husband fucked me. It wasn't so much the physical feel of it, just the fact that he was taking me like this, the way he always does.

I lay there curled on my side biting the corner of the sheet and keeping my entire body relaxed like the ragdoll I was being.

Clark

The lube is only for that initial penetration. Leonie always gets wet pretty quickly, her cunt lubing itself for me. Occasionally I take her arse, sometimes her pretty mouth. It's up to me but I like fucking her cunt the most.

I was on my knees, rolling my pelvis and bumping against her butt, spearing in and out, making her flesh shudder, holding her hip so I didn't force her over onto her belly yet. This position was good to build up a load, stimulating but not too intense that I'd be in danger of losing it too quickly.

I fucked my woman for a few minutes, until the first tingles started in the base of my balls. I worked her onto her front and shoved a pillow beneath her hips. I straddled her and started thrusting harder, pounding against her arse, slapping loudly and spearing oh so deep into her juicy wet heat.

Leonie was silent and completely relaxed. I took it to the brink and slammed into her to hold firm, right on the verge of erupting but not quite past that point of no return. I was pumped up so hard and sensitive though and I could feel my wife's cunt pulsing as she orgasmed. It was the only sinew in her body active, her tunnel of flesh wrapped around my cock.

I said nothing, just waited for her contractions to fade, then resumed fucking her for my own pleasure. I rode her arse, smacking hard against her and quivering her flesh, spearing deep and giving an extra thrust when fully inside of her pulsating fuck tunnel. I had worked it out beforehand and knew it was too early in her cycle to worry, so when

24

my swollen nuts did fill beyond the point of no return, I remained jammed hard against my wife's arse with my cock all the way up her to empty them.

Leonie just lay there on her belly and accepted my load, her pretty head to one side on the pillow and her eyes open but focused casually on the closed curtains.

I pulled out most of the way and squeezed off, slapping her gooey cunt open within her thigh gap. I grabbed a few tissues and dabbed them against her opening. One of her hands appeared from beneath and she took over. I left her to it and gave my cock a wipe then put on my pyjama shorts and got into bed.

I spooned in behind. Leonie peered back and met my kiss. "Night," she said.

"Night baby."

*

The yacht was a twin-engine diesel-powered vessel, no actual sails to worry about. We boarded in the rain, that only got worse as we headed south a kilometre offshore then gradually east and out to sea. There was a low-pressure system up in the tropics, with the tail of it lashing southward. Our first day was spent entirely indoors, playing cards and making the most of an unfortunate situation.

We men had agreed on who was sleeping where. Linus took the one sleeping berth. There was originally another but that had been converted to refrigeration space, as a lot of the charter work Dirk took on was deep-sea fishing. Dirk and I crashed on lounges in the living area. Dirk relieved young Santos at the helm in the early hours, keeping up our five knots through the night and having us well into our crossing of the Tasman Sea.

Days two and three were grey and miserable too, with the weather ranging from light drizzle to heavy showers and some quite severe squalls. Again it was good to be on a powered boat and cruising along without incident at a good steady rate. It was most unfortunate for Linus and Victoria, as their only reason to be sailing at all was to enjoy the experience, which required nice weather really.

There was a break in the cloud cover on day four, allowing for some time up on deck and enjoying the whale watching and the pods of dolphins. "Oh my god, look at them all!" Leonie cried, gripping and shaking my arm. We had come across a super-pod of hundreds of dolphins, no doubt feasting on an abundance of fish in the area. The ocean had become calm and almost glassy as we sailed away from another sunset.

On day five, only two days out from our refuel stop, we finally got it. Brilliant sunshine, light breeze and a glassy calm ocean. Dirk was at the helm, as usual, for the morning shift. He did seven hours as captain morning and afternoon. Young Santos took over steering the boat for two five-hour shifts either side of midday and midnight.

This was the first time Leonie was able to lose the jacket and get some sun. She came up the stairs in white shorts and a little pink tube top, her nipples on show through it. "Is this alright, do you think?" she asked me privately. "Victoria didn't seem to care, and she's only got a bikini top on herself."

"No, you look fantastic, baby. Always!"

"Hmm, but this isn't too skimpy? Not too revealing?"

I swallowed. "I don't think anyone's going to complain if Victoria didn't."

Leonie giggled. "Yes I'm sure." She plucked at her tube top, tugging it down. It didn't cover her belly at all, just a broad band of pink around her boobs. You could see her nipples quite clearly through the thin fabric.

Linus came up the stairs and edged past us, leaning in for a good morning half-hug and cheek kiss with Leonie. "Ah yes, very pretty," he commented about what she was wearing. "Finally some skin!" he tossed back cheekily and headed for where his wife was sunbathing on a lounge to the rear of the top deck.

I squeezed Leonie's shoulders. "Well he certainly doesn't mind."

"Hmm and should I go say hello to Dirk like this?" my wife asked teasingly. "He said to me earlier that it's a nice day to sunbathe. I think he's hoping I might."

I nodded and swallowed again. "Yeah I'm sure he is."

"Uh huh." My wife squirmed back against me down below. "Mmm I'm so horny Clark, I wish we had a bedroom of our own right now."

"Yeah me too, baby. Can't even jack off unless I did it in the shower or whatever. I can't wait till we get to port in a couple of days."

"I know. I'm sure these other men are feeling it too, unless they do it in the shower, do you think?"

"No, I don't know. I've never tried it in a shower. Doesn't sound very appealing to me."

"Hmm, me either. I need your tongue, Clark. That and Buzzy!"

I laughed. Buzzy is our name for a sucking, vibrating clit stimulator I keep charged up for whenever Leonie wants me to go down on her. "We'd be able to hear it all through the boat if you tried that in the shower, baby."

We were cuddling and watching the ocean. Leonie leant back against me, my arms around her and her hands over the back of mine on her bare belly. Linus strolled by again, this time with empty glasses and headed for the bar at the outdoor kitchen. He'd laid out food in preparation for barbequing our lunch. This was our first chance to have a party on deck.

He strolled past again with fresh cocktails for him and his wife. His eyes flashed to Leonie's nipples but only for an instant.

"Okay baby, so there's no way around letting these guys enjoy a perv at you. There's a great view of your tits through that top, or your nipples at least, and it doesn't leave much to the imagination. But it depends which tops you wear and I wouldn't expect you to cover up at all. I can handle it, the way you're pulling the looks. You know I'm pretty well used to it."

Leonie took a breath and expelled. "You're used to it, huh? It's not still exciting for you then?"

"Um, no, I didn't mean it that way," I explained quickly. "I meant I'm used to other guys looking, not that it doesn't excite me when you dress like this."

"Hmm okay, so it does excite you when I dress like this. That's good. But why does it, Clark?"

"Huh, that's easy. Because you're hot, baby." I kissed my wife's pretty hair. "You have an amazing body, Leonie. It would excite any red-blooded man seeing you in a skimpy top. Me included."

"Hmm I see. And it's not complex at all? It's as simple as being pleasing to look at?"

"Bit more than pleasing," I corrected.

"Yes, but it's simply about you enjoying a look, is it? There's no added complexity when other men look at me too?"

"Um yeah…" I felt my face flush. "Yeah there's added complexity, baby. Of course there is."

"Yes, and is that added complexity also a source of excitement for you?" my wife asked, peering up at me and smiling expectantly, I thought. "I know it makes you crazy for sex. I don't understand it, but I know how you always fuck me so nice and demanding anytime I wear one of these tops."

I felt myself flushing guiltily now. There's no doubt that was the truth but, "I don't understand myself, baby. I don't know why it gets to me like that either."

"Hmm I thought as much." My wife smiled broader. "So in that case I want to tell you one thing, then ask you one thing. That okay?"

"Oh yeah, sounds ominous."

"Maybe," Leonie teased. "Are you ready? Okay... Well I can tell you that our hosts might be a little kinky themselves. Victoria was telling me in bed last night that she wants to get Dirk involved in a game of strip so she can have a look at 'what he's packing'."

I gulped. "At 'what he's packing'?"

"That's what she said, word for word. And apparently a big reason for them financing most of this yacht was so she could get that look, if not more! Although I'm making that up a little bit. She didn't say she wanted to have sex with him, I'm just assuming."

"Right. So Victoria has the hots for their charter yacht guy." I tilted to look ahead at where Dirk was at the helm, steering from top deck today in such nice weather. "I suppose women would find the guy alright to look at," I surmised.

My wife tilted to look too. "Yes, to put it mildly." She looked to me teasingly. "I'm just saying!" She had another look. "I mean he obviously looks after himself and he's got that rugged handsome thing going on. Poor me and Victoria don't stand a chance!"

"Oh yeah?" I asked. I didn't really need to feign being wounded by that. "Are you saying just him?"

"Oh, we want to look at you too silly. Actually that's the thing I wanted to tell you. Not that Dirk is an attractive man, but that Victoria is actually serious about organising a game of strip to get him to take his clothes off."

I experienced a flush of nervous excitement and thought that through quickly. Obviously it wouldn't only be Dirk playing this game of strip.

"Okay, so when does she want to do that, baby?"

"Um tonight, when Santos is busy at the helm. She said she'd be too mortified if she had to undress herself in front of a teenager, but she'd be fine with you and Dirk. She's got a pretty good body for her age."

"Yeah I noticed," I said, kissing the top of my wife's head and having to hold her wrists to stop her from pinching and tickling me.

"Oh you think so, do you? And you've obviously noticed!"

"Haha, not until today in her bikini. She's rocking that, looks great," I said more seriously. "But would that mean

33

us playing strip too, like *you* playing and having to strip for Dirk and Linus if you lost?"

"Um…" My wife grimaced up at me. "So, you can see the question I wanted to ask you."

"Ah I see. And how serious is this? Do you think Victoria would really try to make it happen?"

"She's mentioned it about five times. I think her fantasies about Dirk are the reason they're here, and I think Linus knows it and is either onboard, if you'll pardon the pun, or willing to turn a blind eye and let his wife indulge at least." Leonie looked up at me again. "Although I don't know how far he'd be willing to allow her to indulge, if you know what I mean."

I took a big breath and expelled. "Right… And so I guess the question, like you said, is whether or not I'd be okay if you had to strip."

"Uh huh, and whether I'd be okay if you had to," Leonie added and looked back up at me again. "I'm not sure I want this Victoria bitch dreaming about my man the way she obviously does about other men."

34

"Oh okay. Good to know," I said, sort of chuffed to hear that. But I had a sudden flash of guilt about the same in reverse. "The thing about that is though, baby, I was actually going to ask if you wanted to try going topless again this trip, so maybe I'm letting us down in terms of being protective of our relationship, yeah?"

"Um no, I was going to ask you the same thing," Leonie explained quickly. "I was wondering if you'd like me to do it again with Dirk. I think I'd like to if you didn't mind."

I flushed hot up my neck and face again. I stroked my wife's hair and down her neck. "No, I guess I wouldn't mind, baby." I took a breath. "I mean, either swimming again or even if it was playing strip. I'd be okay with Dirk getting another look at your tits, or if this old guy does too. I'm sure they'd both love it, or even Santos. He is 18 so he's old enough, although he looks young. But definitely old enough to want to look haha. He's got eyes all over you baby, ever since he saw you in your boob top at the marina."

"Hmm, well all I brought is boob tops, so he'll be happy as long as it stays sunny now, I suppose."

I stroked down from my wife's bare shoulder and brushed my fingers over her nipple. She caught my hand and covered it, checking from side to side that we weren't being watched. Then she pressed my hand against her tit and held it there whilst lifting back to kiss me over her shoulder. "Mmm you're making me so horny Clark." She was pressing back against me down below again and I firmed up quickly. "Ooh I want you inside me so bad."

"Yeah me too, baby. I wonder if we could both fit in the shower."

We laughed. There was nothing to do but wait though. We weren't about to sneak off into the only bedroom or try and squeeze into the tiny shower for sex. It was only another two days and we'd be calling into a port in New Zealand and spending the night in a hotel room. So we just had to wait.

"Alright, go and say good morning to Dirk I suppose. I'll hang back here and just watch him with you."

"Um okay," Leonie said, facing me now as she checked her top and plucked at it.

"Go on then, go and show him," I said to my wife. "Let him have a look at them in that little top for now and you can show him properly later."

Leonie swallowed and took a breath. She grimaced. "And what should I do when he gets handsy this time? He's always giving me little hugs around the waist and I can't help going weak at the knees when he does it."

"Yeah I've noticed, but you ask for it, baby. It's just your friendly nature and the way you hug everyone. The guy has just picked up on that and plays up to it."

"But I don't hug everyone, do I?"

"Sure you do. Probably without even thinking. You've hugged Linus and Dirk each morning so far on this trip, but you always do that. Not so much with Santos, but that must be a maturity thing. It must only be with adults. Or adult men at least."

"Oh." Leonie grimaced guiltily. "Well I'd probably hug Victoria too, except we've been sleeping together anyway, so no need for a greeting in the morning."

"Yeah baby, I'm sure it's a unisex thing, and it's just your friendly nature like I said. I think Dirk is just making the most of it, and I can hardly blame him if he can get away with an extra squeeze in return."

"Um okay then, I'll just go and um..!" Leonie motioned towards Dirk at the helm. He hadn't even looked back and laid eyes on my wife as yet. She kept checking back and grimacing nervously as she approached him. He welcomed her to his side with a huge smile and she leant into a one-arm squeeze as his eyes rolled down her body and zeroed in on her tits.

I leant on a side rail and averted my gaze out to sea. I kept checking on them and noticed Dirk kept hold around Leonie's waist while they chatted and laughed. Then she took over the wheel while he ducked into the top-deck toilet and washroom. She smiled back at me. She loves steering the boat. We were all having little turns when the weather permitted.

Dirk returned and took hold of her hips at first, then gave her waist another squeeze as she moved aside and let him take over the wheel again. I watched his huge hand clutching around just below her tit, definitely pressing up into it with his thumb, the way he always does. His eyes were zeroed in again too. And that was the last I saw as I headed back down the stairs to conceal the erection in my shorts.

My shorts were stretchy and quite tight-fitting. My cock isn't small and can be a bit too obvious when in a state of arousal. I sat on a couch and opened my computer on my lap. Santos smiled and nodded a good morning as he came from the galley with a sandwich, heading up onto the top deck.

I did some reading and managed to put aside thoughts of my wife being enjoyed by the men upstairs. I ignored both feelings on the matter – the angst and the arousal. I didn't know what to think of my own thoughts and reactions to Leonie being looked at and no doubt fantasised about. She came down and gave me cuddles and kisses, glowing excitedly, as she was.

After Linus's delicious lunch of barbequed lobster and Moreton Bay Bugs with fresh salad and herb dressing, Leonie donned a bikini and spent the day reading and sunbathing whilst the other three men's eyes remained glued to her pretty much the whole time.

Both ladies put on a sunbathing show all day as a matter of fact. Victoria looked great for a woman in her early forties. She's as slender and petite as Leonie. Her tits were not quite so perky but I was certainly hoping to get a look at them if this game of strip eventuated.

The barbeque kind of blended into dinner. Santos had taken over the helm and Dirk was having a few beers with us. He had been measured in his drinking so far and was definitely pacing himself again today. Not so the ladies or Linus. By the time we all headed down into the lounge later that evening, they were giggly and conspiratorially whispering together on one of the couches.

"I think we should play girls versus boys poker!" Victoria announced. "Us two versus you three, losers have to strip!"

The ladies had obviously worked this out together. I'd been waiting for it of course, and Linus didn't look surprised. Dirk was kicked back on a couch with one foot up on the coffee table, his thighs spread open. His package pretty damn full-looking.

"Oh yeah, teams huh? Sounds like fun," he said without looking away from the women and making them both blush.

Linus had been playing cards all the time, Patients on his own or Euchre or Rummy anytime he could talk anyone into a game. He picked up his deck from the coffee table, shuffled and split and twirled the deck around in one hand. "Poker huh? One hand for the ladies and one for us men. We're playing show, are we?"

"Haha it'll be show alright," Dirk said with a chuckle. "Couple of losses and the girls will be showing it all."

"Hmm not fair though. We need rules," Leonie challenged. "There's no one flip-flop at a time for you guys." She looked to her girl partner. "We've only got three articles of clothing each and we'll be showing after two. I say the men have to be showing after two as well."

We all laughed. "Showing what after two?" Dirk asked on behalf of us men.

"Chests after two losses, penises after three!" Victoria declared. "Shorts, shirts then underpants, in that order.

Kick off those flip-flops boys. Come on now, we're playing fair."

We all laughed some more. All three of us men had on footwear so we took them off. Linus removed an Hawaiian shirt. He had a t-shirt on underneath. We were all down to the three items. The ladies were both in bikinis and a wrap with no footwear anyway.

We were seriously going to do this. I was glad to be drunk enough to not bone up prematurely. I felt it flexing a little and tried to talk it down in my head as the cards were readied and the deal began.

Linus turned up two sets of five cards. It was to be simple poker. The ladies had a pair of threes, pointing together to keep them. We men conferred and agreed on keeping an ace and queen.

"Okay ladies first," Linus announced.

He turned over a six and they sighed, then a king and they sighed again, then a ten and they groaned and complained the deck was rigged.

"It's not fair, you're cheating!" Leonie accused playfully as Linus turned us over a ten, then a jack.

"Oh yeah go the king!" I called out.

"No don't cheat!" Leonie squealed as Linus turned over our final card, which was a six, making the ladies jump up and down together squealing and laughing at how they'd beaten us with a lowly pair of threes.

"Come on, off with your pants!" Victoria demanded. "Come on all three of you. No excuses!"

We men all stood chuckling and shrugging to each other. We each dropped our pants and stepped out of them. The ladies cheered. Linus was in white boxers. I was in predominately red briefs, Dirk's were black and at least as full as mine, if not a little fuller.

There was a definite tenting of Linus's boxers as he sat and gathered and shuffled the deck of cards. "Alright now," he said and turned over five cards for the ladies, four of them hearts. We all shut up and watched as he flipped our five cards, which included a pair of eights.

"It's not great odds you'll draw the fifth heart, ladies. I'd keep your ace and hope for the best," Linus advised.

"Hmm I don't know," Leonie said to Victoria.

"I'm feeling lucky," Victoria shot back.

The girls shrugged together. "We're going for the flush," they announced in unison and Victoria turned the odd club they had face-down.

"Alright," Linus warned, shaking his head. "Should we do ours first, leave your one card draw for a big finale?"

"Yes, yes, do yours first!" Leonie enthused. "Let's see what you get."

Linus covered our three discards, drawing another eight to give us three of a kind, and rubbish otherwise.

The ladies were forward in their seats, eyes wide and hands clenched together. None of our three from the top of the deck had been a heart. Dirk did a drumroll on the coffee table. Linus turned over the king of hearts for the ladies. They shrieked.

"Damn it, couldn't have rigged the deck for us, man!" Dirk complained to Linus. We three men all shook heads at each other and stripped our shirts to the cheers and shrieks of the ladies.

Linus had a spare tyre around his waist. I haven't got any fat on me but I'm not ripped or anything. Dirk's chest and stomach were a total washboard. Both Victoria and my wife had shut up shrieking and sat there gawking. We had seen Dirk shirtless swimming last year of course, and sure he was fit-looking but I didn't remember him being as deeply chiselled as this. He looked like he was carved from granite.

Linus shuffled the cards again. "Alright lads, we're going to need a turn-around here. Fingers crossed, yeah!"

He laid out five cards for the girls, three discards and a pair of aces. "Shit," he grumped. The girls just sat there smiling with glazed eyes looking back and forth from their two aces to Dirk's washboard. It looked like there was a bulge to one side in his jocks.

Linus laid out our five cards, including a pair of queens. "Alright go the queens," Dirk cheered. I swallowed hard. Linus took a breath and turned over three more discards for the girls.

They sighed.

"We've still got them," Victoria encouraged Leonie.

Linus flipped us a three, a six, then as Dirk did his drumroll again, Linus turned us up a third queen.

"Oh yeah!" Dirk cheered, I was fist-pumping. Linus started a slow clap.

The ladies were smiling their heads off as they each pulled at the ties in their wraps and undid them, opening to reveal that they both had erect nipples. Leonie's poked at her red bikini top and Victoria's poked at her gold trimmed white one.

"Ooh yeah, fucking beautiful," Dirk said, looking from one woman to the other, both of whom were still doe-eyed whenever they looked at his chest and stomach. The brash confidence evaporated from Victoria's smirk and my wife gawked like she wanted to have the guy's babies.

"Alrighty then, lets get those bikini tops off eh, lads!" Linus declared, shuffling the next hand.

"No, lets just have turns now. You guys are next!" Leonie tried laughingly, raising a raucous protest at changing the rules now that she was in danger of losing.

"Well let me get us some more wine then darls, give us some strength yeah?" Victoria said.

"Hey sweetie hurry back." Linus paused and waited a minute until Victoria returned with another bottle of red.

46

She opened it and poured two large wine glasses and the ladies both took several quick sips.

"It's all in the cards now," Linus told Victoria, and he proceeded to turn them over. There was absolutely nothing worth keeping, all small cards, mixed suits, no pairs and too big a spread to attempt to make a straight. "Yes, now we're cooking," Linus went on and flipped us men three jacks.

"No way!" Leonie cried. "This is rigged. We've been played Victoria. How could you be married to this man!"

"I know right! Hand them over," Victoria demanded.

We men were all laughing. Linus handed over the cards.

Victoria covered their five with another hand of nothing and tossed the deck on the table, huffing and shaking her head.

"Come on, off with those bikini tops. Let's see some tits!" Dirk cheered.

Linus was still laughing. I shut up, suddenly faced with the fact my wife was about to show these other men her perfect little boobs.

"Oh fuck yes," Dirk groaned approvingly as Victoria lowered her top and showed us her firm-looking little globes with lovely pink areola and longish nipples that looked in need of sucking.

We all looked at Leonie. She untied the knot behind her neck and lowered her bikini top, showing her perky tits and highset eraser style nipples, quite red compared to Victoria's and only small but also very nice to suck on and nibble.

"Fuck yeah there they are," Dirk groaned low and appreciably as he reached across and wound one of Leonie's bikini strings around a finger. He pulled it from her completely, making her arch forward and thrust her tits at him and Linus.

We were all quiet now. We were wide-eyed and looking furtively about, wondering what was next. Dirk seemed different, more calm and in control than I felt, that's for sure.

"Okay enough with the games, let's get these panties off too before I have to go relieve the boy at the helm." He looked to Linus, motioning to Leonie. "Do you want to get hers and I'll um…" He motioned to Victoria for himself.

The women said nothing. No protest, nothing. I just gulped hard and stayed shut up too. Dirk took hold at Victoria's hips and Linus took hold of my wife's bikini pants at her hips. The girls both lifted their butts as their pants were stripped from them. They were giggling and hanging onto each other's hand.

"Okay fine. Your turn now!" Victoria told us men, Dirk in particular. She was trimmed almost bare, her slightly protruding labia looked pink and inviting. Leonie has a landing strip, her pussy waxed otherwise. Her thigh gap was broader than Victoria's and there was a fine view of the length of her slit for Dirk and Linus to enjoy.

They were both standing then lowered their underwear together, cocks springing free. The ladies shrieked and glared wide eyed at Dirk's huge dong. I quickly pushed my jocks down and took them off. Victoria had a look at my cock, then smiled up from it with her brows raised appreciably.

Things had gotten quiet again. There were some oohs and aahs and the girls ended up doing as much staring as us men were. Linus got up to get us more drinks, his good-sized member proudly leading the way. Dirk was bantering with Victoria about the possibility of doing adults-only cruises with their yacht, now they'd obviously dropped their standards of decorum. He was absently holding his cock upward and tugging his balls from between his powerful-looking thighs. He let go of his package, leaving it fully on display for the ladies now. They were both pink in the face, virtually licking their lips and rubbing their hands together, or so I imagined in my head.

My wife was all doe-eyed again. She was definitely up for having this man's baby, the magnificent physical specimen that he was. You could see her subconscious mind ticking over, her body knowing what it needed and no doubt preparing itself. Dirk was constantly checking on them, tilting one way and the other to look at both women's cunts.

I looked over at where Linus had decided to stay out of it, back at the bar just watching on. He nodded to me, did a little wink and a toast with his glass. He had taken his shorts with him. I grabbed mine and walked around the back of my couch to join him without disrupting what was happening between my wife and this pumped-up alpha male.

Dirk was definitely the alpha in the room now that we had our clothes off. Neither Linus nor I measured up in that sense. He had our wives giggling like a couple of schoolgirls, both having lifted their wraps and covered themselves with them. There was still the flashing of tits and you could angle for a look between their legs, but it seemed the game of strip was over for everyone except Dirk who remained naked.

But he had to leave. We were apparently crossing a shipping lane over the next few hours and he needed to be at the helm for that. He left the ladies huddled together with their eyes wide and fixated upon his bare arse as he strolled past Linus and I. He was still butt naked. He casually slung his clothing over his shoulder as he walked.

He gave us a wink. "I'll leave you gentlemen to tend to your wives then, shall I?"

Leonie

Victoria and I leant right over together as our heads tilted to savour every wiggle of Dirk's firm little butt as it disappeared up the stairs.

Our husbands watched us, chuckling together.

"That's it, bedtime for me," Victoria announced, and she left me with a squeeze of my hand and a kiss on the cheek. "Good night sweetie, you can thank me for that tomorrow."

I was sure I could smell her arousal. I could definitely feel mine.

Linus kissed his wife at our bedroom door and went into his single berth. Clark approached and slumped onto the couch beside me. I had claimed my bikini bottoms. Clark had brought my top back from where Dirk had left it dangling over the bar on his way out.

I didn't quite know what to say to my man and was too drunk to think clearly anyway. He pulled me to him and took a kiss. He was obviously very drunk too. "Okay, this is my bed right here," he said about the couch we were

52

sitting on. "Unless you want to try doing it in the shower with me? I know I'd be up for it after that, baby."

"Hmm me too, but I think I'd better just go to bed and sleep it off," I said into another kiss, getting up and pushing away from the groping hands under my wrap. "Hold that thought okay? You can take it out on me when we get to port."

"Haha you bet I will, you little hussy!"

I glared back from the bathroom door. I was going to have to try this at least. I was completely slick between the legs and needed an orgasm.

I shut myself in the tiny plastic cubicle and rocked back against the wall. I stuck a hand up the front of my wrap and frigged myself thinking about how it would feel to have my bare boobs pressed against Dirk's chest, his stomach against mine, his little butt thrusting between my legs.

Oh this is so disloyal to my man sitting out there right now but... "Uh huh huh," I moaned as my orgasm clenched and thumped through my body.

I clung to the shower handrail as my legs buckled. I ended up curled in a ball on the shower floor, my head woozy and spinning.

I closed my eyes for a while then pulled myself up and snuck to the bedroom, slipping into bed with the lightly snoring older woman I would definitely have to thank tomorrow.

*

As for tomorrow, our sixth day at sea, I spent it hung over and feeling really quite ill. The ocean had a pretty big swell going and it was all I could do to keep food down and not throw up everywhere.

Clark was doing it tough himself and Victoria was less than her outgoing self. It was left to our crew to get us all safely through our sixth night and into port at a small fishing town on the northern tip of New Zealand.

There was a tourist strip and a line of low-level holiday units along the foreshore. We had booked into one of those, staying two nights, getting our land legs back and enjoying some privacy. It was nice to be finally getting the opportunity to get some much needed exercise happening.

I was feeling miles better by the time we got back to the room after sharing a meal with our fellow tourists and yacht crew. I had been feeling guilty for masturbating in the shower on the boat and decided I'd be allowing Clark to go first.

He had his bottle of lubricant out, placed in full view on the wash basin in our bathroom. I looked from it to his eyes in the mirror, bit my lip and smile and went to bed to wait for him.

I lay with my legs tucked up and my bare butt facing the bathroom. He walked by and lifted the bedclothes, folding them back over me, exposing what he wanted.

I lay clutching the sheet beneath my chin, listening intently but not spoiling it by turning to see what he was doing. I heard the fizz of a bottle of soda water being opened and the sound of Clark drinking. I saw his shadow and felt the cool whisp of breeze against my pussy as he walked past the bed and into the bathroom again. I heard the cap of his oil bottle popping open and the squish of him lathering his cock with the oily lubricant.

Then I held my breath as I felt my husband kneel on the bed behind me. There was the feel of him probing me and then, "Ahh huh huh.." I moaned as he penetrated me and slammed against my arse.

***

Part 2: Leone Wants to go Topless

Clark

My wife lay on her side with her legs tucked up while I fucked her. She was completely wet. I was enjoying deep slow strokes, holding her open by the arse cheek with my thumb watching my cock slide in and out. She was staring at the hotel room wall, expressionless, her eyes glazed. I built my load slowly.

It had been a week since the last time I came and my balls were heavy and getting heavier. I kept slow-fucking my motionless wife until they were full and about to erupt. Then I pulled out and crawled up her body, straddling her and lifting her head, turning it toward me. I stuck my cock in her mouth.

She stared at me while I emptied my balls, dutifully swallowing but otherwise remaining completely relaxed. Like a doll. I grunted my satisfaction but said nothing, as were the rules of our game.

I slumped onto my back on the bed, spent. Leonie turned onto her back too, swallowing again and staring up at the ceiling.

We lay there together without exchanging a word whilst my breathing settled. Hers had remained calm and regular. After about five minutes she got up and went to the ensuite for a drink of water. When she returned she placed one of her toys on my stomach, her favourite. It was her clit stimulator. I took hold of it as she straddled my head and lowered to cover my mouth with her wet open pussy.

I dutifully licked and ate into her, sucking on her folds and baring my teeth for her to rub her clit against. She grabbed a handful of my hair and rode my face. It wasn't long until she ground into me and orgasmed.

Her slender body convulsed and her juices filled my mouth and senses. She remained straddling my face until the first wave passed then she dismounted and pulled me by the hair as she rolled onto her back spreading her legs. I turned over and shifted lower, kissing and sucking her inner thighs. I turned on the stimulator whilst splitting her cunt open with two fingers. I dialled up the vibration as I placed the hollowed rubber tip over her clit.

Within seconds my wife bucked and cried out, her fingers twisting in my hair. I held the clit stimulator in place and nuzzled in under it to lick into her. She let go of my hair and gripped the bedclothes either side of her hips that writhed up off the bed as her beautiful body tensed and resumed convulsing and flinching in orgasm.

I kept servicing her for thirty minutes, taking her through half a dozen peaks before she started giggling and became too sensitive, pushing the stimulator away. Too sensitive even for my tongue now. Her body trembled and continued to clench uncontrollably.

I was fully erect again. I gave her a minute to settle then got on top of her. She was so wet and open as I slammed my cock into her ragdoll body and fucked her hard until I was ready to nut again. Then I lurched up over her, held her by the hair and emptied my balls into her mouth again.

"Nyaa fuck yeah," I snarled down at her. She stared blankly up at me, her eyes wide and glazed, her slender neck gulping as she swallowed.

I squeezed off the last of that much-needed release then flopped down beside my woman again. We both lay staring up at the ornate ceiling, both sweaty and measuring breaths. I sought her hand and she slipped it into mine.

"Do you need another drink?" I asked after a while.

"No I'm fine." She swallowed. "That second one wasn't as strong."

"Right. I was banked up for that first one."

"Uh huh, I noticed." My wife turned her head, biting her lip. "It was a big mouthful. I hope Dirk and Santos are getting a release too. It must be really hard for you men with no privacy on the yacht. I can imagine how much they'd both be banked up too."

"True. It's not the same doing it for yourself either, unless they meet a woman while we're here I suppose. I don't know if there'd be any massage places or whatever."

"Yes, Happy Ending House. Haha. There should be one at a port like this, with men arriving from weeks at sea. You'd think there'd be working ladies to see to their needs."

"Yeah I guess. It's a serious port when you look at the ships docked. There's probably lots of men away from home looking for company for a night or two."

I took the clit stimulator into the ensuite and cleaned it then put it on the charger. Leonie cuddled up when I got back into bed and we enjoyed our first night sleeping together in a week.

The next day was a stopover. We met up with our travel companions and decided to do a trail ride. Leonie grew up riding horses and Linus and Victoria have a farm with some of their own. I don't mind the occasional pony ride. And this was all about getting some exercise and enjoying something other than the endless ocean.

We joined a large group of fellow tourists on a local trail ride. The ride took us through dense, deep green forest filled with some amazing looking ferns, including Pongas, so we were told. The underside of the Ponga leaves are silver. 'That's the symbol for the Kiwi footy team, the silver fern', our guide proudly announced. I imagined he must have been a Maori with his broad flat nose and a Moku tattooed on his chin.

We ascended slowly through the damp, musty-smelling forest, listening to the amazing sounds of the birdlife. One of our fellow riders spotted a beautiful red-beaked bird flying just up ahead. It had amazing indigo plumage that flashed at us as he flew off. "Yeah, that's the Takahe, and if you listen for a minute you'll hear the Tui singing to us. Oh there's one, see that little black bird sitting on the branch up there, looks like it's got a parson's collar on its neck."

After being serenaded for another half hour by the beautiful singing from the Tui's we eventually came to a clearing. And suddenly we had a fantastic view of the cliffs and jagged rock formations dotting the shoreline of the small harbour. There was a broad shipping lane out to sea, the direction we would be sailing tomorrow morning, north up into the tropics.

From a lookout atop the cliff face the trail took us into a small village and to a farm that was set up to provide our lunch. It offered a small petting zoo and a rather impressive bird sanctuary. When our guide noticed us all admiring one of the birds he said: "Yeah that's the Kea, the most intelligent bird in the world. But you gotta watch your windscreen wipers, they like to pinch the rubber to put little rooves over their nests to make 'em waterproof".

My wife spun around and whispered in my ear: "Do you think he's having us on?"

"Haha, he's a bit of a character. I have heard Kea's are extremely intelligent, actually I've seen them being experimented on and I wouldn't put it past them to build waterproof rooves, haha."

"Yeah well it seemed pretty damp in the forest so they must get a bit of rain," my wife responded with a giggle.

As we slowly wandered around a little further we came to a pig pen. I cuddled in behind my wife as we watched the pigs. They rolled around in the mud at first then one started nudging another one's belly. Its ears shot bolt upright, its eyes widened and its body became tense and completely motionless. "Uh oh," I teased Leonie, knowing what was about to happen here.

"Oh my!" Victoria cried as she came up beside us. The huge hairy boar had mounted the pig standing stock-still. It thrust urgently, its huge corkscrew penis probing and flailing about until it hit home and the boar settled into place coupled with the sow, who was waiting patiently beneath him.

There were oohs and aahs and a few chuckles from other people watching. I was firming against my wife's butt and she wriggled back against me. "Ohmygod he's huge. How can she take his weight? And he's certainly getting a release, but what about the other one?" Leonie said about a second boar watching on with interest.

There were other female pigs around too, wallowing disinterestedly in the mud. The boar, smaller than the one mating, approached and sniffed then nudged the sow's belly. The boar on top just eyeballed it, too busy ejaculating and drooling to do anything more, by the look of it. It was foaming at the tusks and its huge balls finally clenched tight and pulsated.

"Hell, that's quite the release," I commented as Leonie tilted to look at the animal's balls as well.

"God they must hold a lot though," she said and rubbed her head up against my chin. "Bet the sow's glad she doesn't have to do oral."

"I'll bet she is," I agreed, fascinated by the animal interaction. The smaller boar was getting excited, nudging more firmly almost dislodging the bigger one, who was hanging on tight with its front legs and thrusting again now. It humped and ground against the sow. After another minute or so with its nuts pulsating again, its now long, thin penis slurped out and dangled spent. As the smaller boar continued nudging the sow the larger one slipped off and went over to a water trough for a drink.

The sow still had her ears up and was quivering. The smaller boar mounted, barely able to reach her properly as its penis flailed and probed, but when he hit home he shuffled right up on the tip of his hooves and quickly settled into place. Its balls immediately clenched and began to pulsate.

"Better?" I asked into my wife's hair. I was erect against her butt.

"Phew. Uh huh, that's fair now. I felt so sorry for that small one missing out like that."

I swallowed and took a breath. "Yeah and the sow doesn't seem to mind."

"Hmm she's loving it."

"Oh yeah?"

"Uh huh, as she would with the boys not fighting or anything, just waiting and having turns with her."

"I see. And it's okay for the boys to have turns is it?" I teased into a neck kiss.

"Oh my god!" Leonie cried though. "Oh wow, look at him. He's so huge!"

Another boar strolled out from behind a hay bale and walked towards the sow and the young boar mating.

"Oh he must be older. He's even bigger than that first one," Leonie enthused. "And hairier. And look at those tusks!"

We watched fascinated. The young boar was thrusting urgently now and looking worried. He settled again and resumed ejaculating by the looks, but as the big old boar approached he jumped off and quickly moved away.

The big old fellow sniffed behind the sow where she was leaking semen. Her eyes were wide and rolled back, but she remained standing stock-still with her ears pricked and quivering. The huge granddaddy boar mounted with ease, his powerful haunches holding him up. You could see the sow visibly brace as he relaxed his weight on her back.

"Oh wow, this is getting very naughty now," Leonie said back up at me without removing her eyes from the show these animals were putting on. I suddenly seemed aware that pretty much the whole tour group was lined around their pen.

The grandaddy boar settled into place. His nuts were the size of rockmelons. They clenched up tight and began to pulsate.

I had an arm around my wife and she was cuddling it to her front. My thumb was under her tit and I wanted to rub and have a feel but couldn't with people so close to us. I remained firm against her butt and enjoyed the feel of her deliberately pressing back against me. Others in the group moved along but we watched until the huge old boar eventually hopped off and strolled back over to his hay bale, nuzzling a bed and collapsing onto his side to yawn and close his eyes. The sow rolled in mud and closed her eyes too. Only the young boar was left standing, trying to nudge her to get back up.

"The poor boy, she should have let him have another turn and finish properly," Leonie said as we wandered away.

"Yeah it kind of seemed that way, didn't it," I agreed. "When you look at it like that just naturally. Although the sow might have been tired from standing like that for so long with all that weight on her."

"Yes, although the big old one could have waited for the little one to finish. Scaring him off like that when he was obviously still.. you know…"

I chuckled. "Yeah they were probably still half full, the size of the damned things."

"Mmm maybe." Leonie lifted to whisper as we walked. "Are yours getting full again yet?"

"Yep, will be by tonight."

"Mmm okay. I almost wish they were as big as a boar's now after watching that."

"Haha yeah, or if there were three sets of them for you to drain," I teased, giving her a bit of a tickle.

My wife laughed. "Yeah I wish!" she teased back at me.

"Oh you wish, do you?"

"Hmm, well I wouldn't mind if I were to be nice and help out like that sow did. Being the only female ready and with three male piggies all needing it."

We had arrived back at the ponies, ready for the descent back down the mountain.

I gave my wife a little cuddle while we waited for everyone to join us. I stroked her hair and kissed her head. I wasn't sure how serious she was about her last statement. I remembered what she had said this morning about our yacht captain and his deckhand.

"Well hopefully Dirk and Santos found themselves a girl each, like you said baby."

"Yes hopefully. I don't like the idea of them taking us on this whole long voyage away from any girls they know." Leonie fiddled with my shirt in front. "It would be so unfair when we go back out to sea for another two weeks now if they haven't had a woman to help them in that way."

I swallowed hard, my heart thumping. "Do you think," I said.

Leonie peered up.

I touched her face and rubbed across her bottom lip with my thumb. "Would you want to help them, baby? I mean just in your mouth?"

My wife nodded a little, her blush rising. "I wouldn't mind that, Clark. Just in my mouth, if they needed to."

I nodded too and took another breath. "Yeah I guess it could be something for all of us while we're out to sea and without much privacy. If it was just oral and I did that for you." I stroked my wife's pretty hair from her forehead. "And if you were doing it for me, and Dirk and Santos as well. Like, just once a day I guess."

"Mmm I guess. Or even more than once if they needed it," my wife breathed into a kiss. "Santos is only young. You know what 18-year-old boys are like."

"Yeah true. As soon as you did it once, he'd be hopeless. He'd be following you around all day like that little boar wanting you to do it again."

"Mmm but it's only a little mouthful from you men. A bit of a strong taste sometimes, but I'd be okay with that, and to let them enjoy watching me swallow each time."

"Aw hell baby, that's so fucking sexy! And you'd let them watch you swallow huh?"

"Hmm of course. I know how much you guys love that. And like with the helpful lady piggy, it's only semen – whether it be yours or someone elses," my wife teased over her shoulder as she walked away.

We mounted our ponies. I had to leave the discussion for now with my seemingly willing wife. It was an interesting idea though. I wasn't certain but I thought I might be okay with it – being able to stand back and allow or even watch Leonie sucking someone else off.

Dirk had already seen her tits and pussy. It was only a matter of time until the ladies were removing their bikini tops and not worrying about young Santos seeing them. It was going to be an awful long few more weeks if I wasn't getting any alone time with my wife, and the idea of her or possibly even Victoria allowing these other men oral sex – well it didn't seem that outrageous crammed together on a small yacht in the middle of the ocean.

We never spoke about it again on the ride down the mountain, and we ended up having afternoon drinks with

Linus and Victoria, then ordering a huge seafood platter to share on their hotel room balcony.

By the time the sun had disappeared we were all a little drunk. We relaxed back watching the lights of the harbour, chatting and laughing together.

"Anyway, I wouldn't mind orally seeing to Dirk sometimes," Victoria blurted suddenly.

Leonie glared at her.

"Oh don't worry sweetie. Linus and I have talked about worse, haven't we Smokie!"

Linus toasted with his wine glass. "Nothing wrong with a bit of spice, I always say."

Leonie looked from one of our travel companions to the other. "Oh my god, you've already talked about it?"

"Well sort of," Linus went on. "After the game of strip the other night. I'd be surprised if that didn't break the ice and make everyone curious for more."

I was feeling no pain with any of this now and had been mulling it over all afternoon. "Nothing wrong with a bit of kinky, is what I always say."

Everyone laughed. "A bit of kink huh?" Linus queried.

I shrugged and wasn't sure if I should say anything but I was too drunk to pull up. "Yeah we do submissive, don't we baby? That's our flavour of kink in the bedroom."

Leonie stared blushing, her eyes wide and rolling away guiltily as she sipped her wine.

We all laughed some more. "Which of you is the submissive?" Linus asked.

"We take turns. I'm hers to command anytime she wants it," I told our new friends.

"Ooh nice!" Victoria said, clapping then rubbing her hands together. "And he does as he's told, does he, sweetie?"

Leonie nodded. "Yes he does. I have to push him off sometimes because I can't take it anymore. It's wonderful."

"Ah perfect. What a good boy you are," Victoria said to me. "Or a good man I should say. Not a selfish boy at all by the sound of it."

"No not until it's my turn and Leonie lies there and lets me do what I want. Then I'm a selfish enough boy."

We all laughed again. "Just lies there?" Linus queried.

"Yes she's my dolly. My hot little ragdoll," I told him while holding my wife's eyes and she blushed.

"Which I can't help, as soon as he touches me," she defended. "I've never been able to resist when a man touches me though."

"Oh really?" Victoria asked with interest.

Leonie looked to her and took a big breath. "I don't know, I just go all weak at the knees and can't even move when a man wants me." She looked to me. "It's so good to be married and only have my husband to worry about like that."

My phone jingled in my pocket. I checked the message and frowned. "What is it?" Leonie asked.

"It's Warwick Kendall. No luck getting our application reconsidered, he says." I looked to our travel companions. "That's the new sonar equipment the university won't let us use unfortunately. It's there at their site just around the goddam corner from where we want to go, and it's doing nothing. It'd be so easy to lend to us. It's a tiny portable device and a laptop. They're just being anal about it."

74

"Ah and it's equipment you need to find this wreck?" Linus asked. "Can't we find one elsewhere and hire it?"

Linus saying 'we' and including himself as part of the expedition was exciting. I did find another device but would have had to purchase it and that wasn't in the budget. "No, I'm sure we can make do with the equipment we have." I didn't want to stretch the friendship here and it was too late, we were only two days sail from the island. "I've got coordinates that will get us close, and our regular sonar should do the rest. Find us a sunken treasure!" I said, cuddling my wife close and meeting her kiss.

"Ah a sunken treasure! How exciting!" Victoria enthused.

"Yes, we hope," Leonie said. "Although finding this particular wreck would be treasure enough, right Clark?"

"Yes definitely. Proving it's there and writing some history. Not to mention the told-you-so factor and shoving that in the Vice Chancellor's face."

We poured more wine and carried on chatting about shipwrecks and moved onto the modern cruise ships Linus and Victoria regularly sailed on, how different that was from sailing on a small yacht.

Our small yacht was apparently fully restocked and refuelled ready for the morning. Once back in our hotel room for the final night ashore I kissed my wife back against our closed door and felt down her panties, rubbed into her enough to moisten her pussy and inserted two fingers up her.

Leonie immediately submitted, resting her head forward against my shoulder while I fingered her and freed my cock. I had her wet enough and inserted and thrust up into her, banging her against the door.

I hooked one of my woman's legs over my arm and held her upright and spread. I fucked her like that for my own pleasure and when I was ready to cum, I quickly pushed her to her knees and emptied my balls in her mouth.

I left her slumped on the floor wiping her mouth on the back of her wrist. I showered and found her sitting on the bed with her clit stimulator in her hand.

She stood and I lay down. She pulled my head around and straddled my face. She was soaked and so hot inside.

She kept a hold of my hair and ground and squirmed against my mouth as I licked and ate into her, lashing and nipping her clit until she bucked and convulsed.

She dismounted my face and slumped on her back on the bed. I picked up the clit stimulator but found it was already wet and slippery.

"It's okay I already did that while you were in the shower," Leonie said, biting her smile. "I did it thinking about that naughty girl piggy and her three boyfriends."

Leonie

They were animals of course, but the idea of being outnumbered by virile men aboard the yacht was intriguing to me. My husband had certainly been worked up for sex after a week at sea and I could only imagine how worked up our powerfully built captain and teenage deckhand would have been.

Actually I had lied to my husband about that last night. I'd used Buzzy while thinking about being the wanton female for three sex-starved men. I'd started thinking about naughty miss piggy but had to go get buzzy when my train of thought drifted to Dirk and Santos, and even to Linus. I loved the way he looked at me. Victoria had told me last night that she doesn't mind him indulging as much as I'm comfortable with, since he's agreed to her having sex with Dirk if she wants.

It was a beautiful summer morning as we sailed out of the pretty, chocolate-box harbour, leaving the northern tip of New Zealand for the open sea again. I was feeling fine, not so my husband who was nursing a hangover. Victoria looked a bit tired too and spent all morning relaxing on deck, laid back in a bikini and sun hat and glasses. Linus served her drinks and snacks. He was always waiting on her. He's so nice like that.

I passed him on the stairs on my way below deck. I was getting changed and glared playfully at him whilst lifting my top on the way into the bedroom. He was still looking back at me.

I went into the bedroom and pushed the door without closing it properly. Not really to invite anyone to peep, but because I didn't expect anyone to walk past as they were all up on top deck right now.

I had a bikini top on under my top. I tossed the top on the bed and got the one from my bag that I was changing into. It was my sexiest one, white and virtually see-through. I had it on the bed and pulled the string behind my back and neck, removing my bikini top.

"Er sorry love," Linus said from the door. "I just needed some more um…" He had a bottle of sunscreen in his hand. There was another one on the dresser behind me.

"Oh okay." I was blushing fully, putting an arm across my breasts. I looked from the bottle to this older man, my naughty ideas ticking over. I took a breath and lowered my arm. He remained there leaning in the open doorway and just looked at my tits. "I thought I might do some sunbathing too, it's so nice up on deck today."

"Yes it certainly is. It's beautiful, love."

Linus looked up from what I was showing him. I had lifted my arms and was pushing back my hair and fixing it in a scrunchie.

79

"Are you going topless? Do you have sunscreen?" Linus asked mildly.

"I thought I might. I was just going to do it up there."

Linus nodded. He edged past me to get the sunscreen. "Or just come up like that, love." He looked at my tits again and smiled. "No one's going to complain."

"Hmm, I'm sure," I said and giggled.

The man had stopped at the doorway again and leant there looking at me. I was blushing to myself as I thought of the next thing to try perhaps. I was in shorts and panties, my bikini bottoms were there in my bag. I lifted them out and sorted them, placing them on the bed.

"It will be nice to see you ladies topless. I'm sure Victoria's only waiting for you to dare to first."

"Yes I know, she said that last night. She's shy about doing it with Santos though."

"Yes we have a son his age, so there *is* that."

I nodded. "But he's not your son, and he's not shy about looking at me and Victoria, if you haven't noticed."

"Haha I've certainly noticed. It's perfectly healthy curiosity and desire from a young man though, nothing untoward."

"Oh definitely! Santos is great. I'm more excited than anything else for him to see me topless." I motioned for the bottle of sunscreen. "Can I um..?"

"Oh of course," Linus said but didn't give me the bottle. Instead his eyes twinkled and he flipped the cap and motioned to my chest.

I bit my smile and thrust my boobs forward. He squirted the cool lotion, a big splotch on one breast then the other. I covered them and rubbed it in before he dared to ask if he could. Judging by the smile on his face he was probably thinking that.

I rubbed down my belly as well.

"That's better love, you wouldn't want to burn them," Linus said and I looked down at my tits with him.

"I know, I did get sunburn the only other time I've done this."

"Ah, well this is virtually total block out. Victoria swears by it."

I held out my hands and got more lotion squirted, applying that to my arms and shoulders. I held my hair aside and turned around. "Please?"

Linus squirted into his hand and smoothed over my upper back and rubbed down the middle and up each side. The feel of his strong hand made me relax and kneel forward on the vanity chair, the one in the room Victoria and I shared. Any man touching me always makes my legs go weak, so it was good to have something to hold onto.

"So that was interesting what you and Clark were saying last night about being submissive for each other," Linus said, looking at me in the mirror and seemingly reading my body, if not my mind. He was softly stroking my back and looked up from my tits. "That's very interesting indeed."

I nodded. I couldn't speak – never can at times like this.

He squirted more lotion and rubbed up my side. I watched him in the mirror. His hand smoothed around and upward, covering one of my tits and making me suck in a breath. "Have to make sure you rub in a little, love. You don't mind if I help, do you?"

I swallowed and shook my head. The older man reached up my front with his other hand and covered that tit as well. I slumped back against him while he felt them and played with my nipples. I was gone, his to do with as he pleased. But there were footsteps coming down the stairs and suddenly Linus was gone from behind me and… "Ah Clark! Are you ready for another shrimp on the barbie?"

Linus had made it obvious my husband was right there, although Clark was headed for the kitchen. I quickly pulled on my top, not sure how wrong it had been, what just happened. Asking a man to put sunscreen on your back whilst topless, alone in your bedroom… well not exactly asking for it, but no surprise he got handsy, I figured.

I wasn't sure where I was up to now with this. I still wanted to go topless for Dirk and Santos. I considered just doing it but chickened out and kept my top on whilst changing into bikini bottoms.

I sat with Victoria and tugged my top up under my oily boobs to sun my belly. Dirk was snoozing. Santos was steering the yacht for his midday shift. Linus and Clark were cooking on the barbeque, Linus glaring cheekily over at me sometimes and making me smile and blush at the flashbacks I got of him feeling me up.

I just can't move when a man touches me. *I'm worse than that lady piggy!*

I went for a stroll to the helm and said hi to Santos. "Can I have a drive?"

He has a huge smile, his teeth brilliant. He's a dark-skinned young guy with big brown eyes. They were down looking over my shoulder as I held the wheel with him close behind me. Of course I can steer without help in the middle of the ocean but I liked the way Santos only ever let me edge in front of him. He was making my nipples hard with anticipation and had them poking at my top, more visible than they already were. I was wondering whether he met a girl back at port and whether she helped him relieve the tension in his balls.

Oh my god I'm a total slut today!

"So did you have fun at the stopover Santos? What did you get up to?"

"Um mostly just restocking and cleaning and that."

"Oh, you didn't get a day off?"

"Na but that's okay. It's good money when you do a trip like this. I like it and I don't care if there's no days off."

"Oh I see. But that makes sense I suppose. It's a holiday for me but it's work for you."

"Yep exactly. That's what the boss always says."

The boy's hand was on my waist. I don't have the same problem, being unable to resist the touch of boys. Only men. I wasn't sure what I'd do if this one got cheeky and lifted his hand from my waist the way Linus had downstairs a little while ago. I was still reeling from that, probably vulnerable to this boy if he tried right now.

I was thinking that as we chatted, imagining him doing it, wishing he would. His beautiful brown eyes were over my shoulder and on my tits the whole time, keeping my nipples so hard they were aching for him to squeeze them.

Clark

I left Linus to the barbeque and went down to the lower bridge to have a play with the spotlight sonar. I turned it on and watched for a while. We were in deep sea and were picking up schools of fish, nothing else. I had a side scan sonar to lower once we reached our destination coordinates. I was going to need good resolution so would be restricted to narrow search lanes. Not easy to find the hull of an ancient timber wreck – sediment in defined lines then pass in several directions to get other angles and build a picture, do some diving. The university had a state-of-the-art side scan device with far superior software, which would detect formations on the sea bed that my equipment could miss. It would remove most of the guess-work from anything I do find, saving valuable time wasted diving for ocean junk or some natural sedimentary formation.

I wondered about Professor Norris – my nemesis of sorts. He was only ahead of me because he was ten years my senior and had had more time to progress. I didn't see him as an intellectual superior or any kind of mentor. He certainly had the Vice Chancellor's confidence and an inside running for anything exciting in terms of research. He would be back at the French wreck by now. There were flights to nearby Tonga and it was only a short days' sail from there with a regular ocean taxi service back and forth.

I wondered if I could somehow negotiate with Norris directly – what it would take to get him onside. I was prepared to offer him a cut in anything we found. But I was more interested in finding the wreck of the Sunline. I didn't seriously anticipate dredging up any sunken treasure, other than a few artefacts.

Norris wouldn't be interested in money either. He was loaded and from generations of family wealth. The only thing I had that he didn't was my lovely wife. I'd seen often enough the way he looks at Leonie, but then again what man doesn't look at her and wish!

Leonie had offered to ask him to help us out but I wouldn't let her. Probably because of how good the guy looks, if I was being honest with myself. Whilst Leonie draws looks from all the men and boys on campus, Professor Norris certainly draws attention from all the women. The young ones fawning after him and the married ones like mine not immune to staring or blushing guiltily away from the guy's smirks.

I went into the storage area in the vacant lower bridge to find the instruction manual for the side sonar I'd hired. I was in the small room and heard Leonie giggle. I leant over and had a look up through a stairwell to the upper deck bridge, where I saw Leonie steering the yacht with young Santos behind her.

He clutched her ribs and made her squirm and shriek. She glared playfully back at him. He did it again and she just scrunched her arm down, not making a sound this time. I saw her eyes roll back but they were glazed now and I knew what that meant. The young guy was watching what he was doing over her shoulder. He wormed his fingers under the bottom of her short tank top. Her arm lifted to give him room as they made their way upward and closed over her tit.

Ohmygod, cheeky little shit...

Leonie remained completely still while this young deckhand felt her up. He was squeezing and kneading her tit and reached around to feel the other one as well. Leonie held the wheel with one hand and lightly held the boy's wrist with her other, keeping her arm raised out of his way.

I was almost directly below them. I could see his package tenting his shorts and pressing against my wife's butt. She was in bikini pants and his bulge was between the cheeks of her butt and she was pressed back against it, or perhaps he was thrusting against her a bit.

He rubbed up her front with his other hand and lifted her top, hiking it above her tits. She only had on the short tank and her tits were bare now.

The young guy's head was still over Leonie's shoulder. I couldn't see their faces at all. I stood mesmerized watching him fondle her tits and play with her erect nipples while she definitely squirmed back against his erect cock. I was fully erect myself and excited for where this was going, but as the boy felt down over Leonie's belly and tried to touch her between the legs, she suddenly snapped out of her typically submissive state and squirmed away. "No I said!" she scolded the boy, letting go of the wheel and making him take over steering the yacht. as he lunged and tried to grab her again she ducked back giggling and pulling her top down to cover her tits.

I backed out of the little storeroom before I was caught spying. This was a surprise, but not a shock. I was thinking it would be Dirk unable to resist taking hold of my wife, not the young deckhand. The way Leonie was dressing and the fact we'd already discussed her potentially doing oral for these men away from home, I was fine with things advancing. I was excited for it and was seriously boned up right now after seeing it begin to play out.

I usually struggled with angst and jealousy when Leonie drew too much attention around campus or at university functions, even just sending her to work with VC Hugo. He's always got his eyes all over her and suggests she should go with him to other cities for seminars for fucking note-taking.

I usually do it tough back at home, but it seemed so different out here in the middle of the ocean. There was something so raw and natural about being out here, and the idea of sharing my woman with these other men seemed fair. It would be selfish and unfair if I didn't. That was what I was thinking And feeling – feeling it in my loins and thinking it with a mind overpowered by the opportunity to live out a long-held sexual fantasy of seeing another man take Leonie in a state of total submission, the way I Is enjoy doing.

I've always wondered what it would be like to watch her being fucked ragdoll by someone else – always wondered if she would just submit the way she does for me. She certainly appeared to be well on the way to submitting to the young deckhand before she snapped out of her trance.

My erection had receded and I headed back up on deck to see about lunch when I saw Dirk pull Victoria into the main sleeping berth and close the door. I had just caught sight of them and briefly met Dirk's glance and wink.

Okay so things are definitely progressing!

I passed Linus coming down the stairs. He looked a bit grim but said nothing. I didn't either, just left him to it as he went to his single berth and closed the door.

Leonie was up on deck and was looking down after where Linus had gone as I approached. "Oh my god, did you see Victoria?"

I took hold of my wife around the waist and looked back down the stairs with her. "I saw Dirk taking her into your bedroom. Is that what it looked like?"

"Yes he was kissing her and feeling her up. He led her away and Linus didn't try to stop him."

"Okay, so it looks like things are definitely hotting up now, baby. I saw you with young Santos. He was getting very handsy with you."

Leonie grimaced with her blush. "You saw?"

"Yeah I was down below." I kissed my wife softly, holding her to me. "I didn't mind. It was pretty hot actually – watching you being felt up like that."

"Mmm was it really? I've decided I don't want to do anything with Dirk though. I'd rather leave him to Victoria."

"Oh yeah? And what about poor old Linus?" I asked into another kiss.

"Hmm, well he felt me up earlier when he was doing my sunscreen for me. So now they've both had a turn at that and made me want to suck them off, if we decide to do that." My wife nibbled my ear and breathed into it as my cock flexed in her hand. "But not until after you do me. I'm so horny for it now Clark. I want to ride your face. Mmm I want you to take me to the bedroom after them and give me lots of orgasms. Then I'll do whatever you want for Linus and Santos, but not for Dirk."

"Haha I'm sure Victoria would be looking after him, baby. I think it's fair to leave him to her."

"Hmm well she's claimed him and she owns the yacht, so best we don't upset her and get left marooned on an island or something for our troubles."

I slipped my hand down the front of my wife's bikini pants, my fingers sinking up into her without resistance. I held her against a wall and finger-banged her to a quick orgasm for now.

Linus came back upstairs and went about preparing lunch. Victoria joined us well fucked and glowing. Dirk took over at the helm and Santos had his eyes fixed upon Leonie as he ate quickly then climbed down into the lower bridge where he had a bunk. Probably to jack off, I suspected.

I wasn't sure of allowing things to progress that far with Leonie yet. I saw her and Victoria talking together quite a bit throughout the afternoon, while Linus was quieter than usual. He seemed to be struggling with the recent events.

I grabbed a book and kept to myself until late afternoon storms closed in around us. We were confined downstairs with card games and too much of the fine New Zealand Pinot Victoria had wheeled onboard by the crate-load.

The next morning the brilliant sunshine was back. I could feel the air getting more humid and tropical now. Linus had sparked up again and was his usual chatty self. The ladies took off their bikini tops whilst sunbathing down the back of the deck. Santos's eyes bulged trying to get looks at them all the while and Linus did the drinks waiting, taking his time whilst serving Leonie.

Again the day was cut short by a summer storm that had us all indoors. I spent most of the afternoon at the bridge with Dirk as he negotiated the swell of the ocean and strong currents on approach to our small island destination.

Leonie

It was night now. I was happy when anchor was finally dropped in a sheltered bay and the boat stopped rocking for the first time in hours. I wasn't a fan of that, or my stomach wasn't at least. We decided to wait until morning to go ashore. We could see lights on the island but it was apparently only a small village and nothing would be open anyway.

I got up through the night and was locked out of the main sleeping berth, so my husband pulled me onto his couch for a cuddle whilst our captain had more sex with the yacht owner.

The bay was calm, the night silent. We could hear Victoria's moans. The light was on in Linus's single sleeping berth. It seemed he was listening too.

His door opened and he came out and sat with us, offering a forced smile after a long look at the closed door where the sounds of Victoria's moans were reaching a crescendo and making me tingle between the legs.

"Apparently he's very well hung," Linus said and drew a big breath, expelling and nodding in apparent defeat. "And has stamina too. Obviously!"

"Yeah man, are you alright though?" Clark asked.

"Oh yes, I'm fine. Doing it hard at the very moment, but it's something we both wanted to try."

"Yeah sure," Clark agreed and kissed my head, keeping me close and stroking my hair. "We've been thinking about it too, haven't we baby? Although not with full sex."

I felt myself blush. I was only in sleep shorts and a tiny crop top that barely covered my boobs. We had sat up and Linus was sitting opposite. I didn't know what to say but just took a breath and lifted off my top.

"Oh!" Linus exclaimed.

I blushed deeper. My husband resumed stroking my hair. I heard him swallow hard. I looked up from my tits to the face of the older man staring at them.

"Yeah we're just thinking about young Santos being stuck out here with no girlfriend all this time, for nearly another three weeks yet," Clark went on mildly. "About maybe helping him out with some oral sex, hey baby!"

I swallowed. "Uh huh maybe."

"Oh my, that would be um…" Linus swallowed hard too, glancing back and forth from the sleeping berth door where all was now quiet.

His eyes lowered to my tits again. I scrunched my shoulders, pressing them together with my upper arms.

"I don't mind that you touched her, man," my husband said evenly and I just about orgasmed. "I don't know if we'd want to go as far as you guys but looking and a bit of touching is okay by me. And she won't be able to move, so long as you don't go too far with her."

"Yes I noticed she submitted immediately when I touched her," Linus said. "I was curious about that. It was extremely arousing to feel a woman do that."

"Ha, tell me about it," my husband said and chuckled.

I was beyond blushing now, my face on fire, my entire body a mass of tingles and my pussy dripping, I could feel it.

"So yeah, if you want to do her suntan again while we're here…" Clark went on and continued stroking hair over my ear. "We're not sure about her doing oral yet. We'll talk about it some more."

"Yes, but you mean oral for the young man?" Linus shot back intently. "You were saying there was a possibility Leonie might do it to ease his suffering, so to speak. Being young and virile, I understand."

My husband took a big breath. "Yeah man, but not only him... I mean depending on what you and Victoria have decided... We weren't just thinking of Santos, were we, baby?"

"Um no, not just him," I answered obediently. "I'd like for all of the men here to be satisfied in that way, and for us women too." I motioned to the sleeping berth door. "I don't see why we shouldn't all be having fun like that," I said encouragingly to my husband.

Clark was right that we hadn't decided anything yet and that we needed to talk some more. I wouldn't have minded sucking Linus off right now though. I felt I could do it right there in front of my husband, and I was sure Victoria would be okay with it, based on what she'd said to me and the fact it sounded like she was probably in no condition to stand up, let alone come out here and complain.

But right then the sleeping berth door opened and Dirk came out pulling on a t-shirt, looking all ripped the way he does, and glistening sweat I would love to have licked off him. He stopped to chat and banter with Linus and Clark about how a week at sea always has the crew and passengers hot for sex. How married or not, male and female, even all male crews most likely deserve their reputation.

I sat quietly with my tits thrust forward for the three men. Linus was still staring at them and Dirk kept glancing and making my pussy drip even more than it already was. Oh my god his package was huge, and I remembered what I saw the other night when we played strip, how damned thick his penis looked even just partially erect.

Linus stood and went to his wife, closing the door behind him. Dirk got a drink of water from the galley and crashed on a couch at the far end of the living area. I cuddled up with my husband and all he did was play with my bare tits, afraid to do anything more with our alpha captain right there facing us in the moonlight.

I couldn't tell if Dirk's eyes were open or not, but when my husband fell asleep, I made sure to keep the sheet we had over us tugged down and my tits available to be looked at.

When I woke in the morning, it was still down and Dirk was still sleeping but young Santos was there sitting on the stairs staring at me.

The boy smiled broadly. I rolled my eyes at him. He was crunching an apple then stood and walked back up the stairs, his firm-looking little butt flexing in tight shorts. *Ooh I wonder if he's been doing it for himself or if he's all banked up and needs me!*

I slipped away from my husband and pulled on my crop top, sneaking past Dirk and up to the galley to make coffee and breakfast. Clark joined me and cuddled behind, feeling up my top and giving my tits a squeeze. "Morning baby, sleep well?"

"Hmm not so much. I'm too horny to think let alone sleep."

"Yeah I know what you mean. It'll be better with Linus and Victoria staying on shore while we're here and us having the double berth. I won't care if Dirk and Santos are listening."

"Mmm me either, but I'm still worried about Santos," I said, turning in the cuddle to try and push this a little bit. "I'm still worried he's missing out and might need me to suck him off, what do you think?" I breathed into a kiss.

My husband kept kissing me, his eyes on mine. He didn't answer but I could see his mind was ticking over and my excitement built. He leant me back a bit to look at. I held his arms and waited. He took a big breath and expelled, nodding to himself, as if deciding to go ahead with some idea or other about this. At least I hoped it was still about sex and the men we were out to sea with.

My husband lifted his gaze to rest upon mine. I knew this look so well. Oh I loved it when he told me what I had to do sexually. I loved it when he just took me and I loved it when he warned me he was going to later. It was just like that – the narrow-eyed gaze and little twinkle of dare.

"You know, baby. I think it would be a fun kind of kinky for you to suck some teenager or older man's cock. But I was also thinking it might actually be a good idea if you come along with me to see the university wreck and maybe I could leave you alone with Norris for a bit – see if you can talk him into letting us use the university's sonar equipment… What do you say?"

I stared back. My mouth had opened but no sound came out.

"I mean, you know what he's like around you baby. If you asked he'd probably say yes."

"Uh huh, maybe," I agreed. My entire body was a mass of tingles again. Oh god was I horny.

"I mean I'm not saying you should do anything with him," my husband went on. "Just that he's got it bad for you, so why not take advantage of that hey?"

I took a breath, gulped and nodded. "Okay," I told my husband. "As long as he doesn't grab me though. You know what will happen to me if he does, Clark. You know I won't be able to move if I'm alone somewhere with Professor Norris and he grabs me!"

The idea of being traded for this sonar equipment had me on the verge of a hands-free orgasm. My husband was fiddling with my hands then a big frown creased his forehead. His eyes still had that glint of dare as they lifted again.

He nodded a little. "Knowing that might happen, would you be prepared to do it, baby? I mean, he might even fuck you, but..?"

The tingles filling me surged and heated my face and pussy at the same time. I bit down on my lip and nodded a little too. "Uh huh, I'd be prepared to do it, Clark. If you take me with you and leave me alone with Professor Norris, I'll ask him nicely for you."

***

Part 3: Leone Gives Oral Relief

Leonie

The island of Mahacu was a tiny remote South Pacific atoll. The main industry was fishing, with a small village settlement that catered to cruise ship tourists. There were twenty or so grass hut style bungalows, mostly empty until the next ship came along. I accompanied Linus and Victoria while Clark stayed aboard the yacht and began his search for the wreck of the legendary HMS Sunline. He was determined to give it a go with the sonar equipment he had. No point demeaning himself and go begging for the state-of-the-art equipment he wanted to borrow from Professor Norris unless he had to.

We checked into our huts first. Ours was next to Linus and Victoria's. They were lovely spacious rooms with all the amenities and the best view of the ocean you could possibly wish for.

I was a bit of a third wheel. Linus and Victoria were holding hands and cuddling up all the time. Victoria looked like a woman who had been thoroughly ravaged, as she had been by our chiselled-from-granite yacht captain the last two nights. Linus was clearly romantically reclaiming his wife. But before he had a chance to re-establish himself as her man she received news of an urgent business matter she had to attend to. So that afternoon we put her on a light aircraft charter flight to Tonga.

"Oh this just isn't fair," I consoled Linus after the plane had taken off and we had done waving.

"No it's fine. It's typical of Victoria's business. I was surprised we weren't called back from New Zealand, although when she checked in with her team they reported all was fine and wished us happy voyaging."

It turns out a major client suddenly pulled out of a fashion parade. Victoria would be able to deal with the problem but needed facetime and reliable internet. You were lucky to get a single bar of reception on your mobile phone here on sleepy little Mahacu.

I hooked my arm in Linus's as we strolled back into the village and around the souvenir shops and little cafés. He had been behaving himself all morning but was looking at my boobs more now. I had on one of my skimpy tops and my nipples were responding to the attention.

There was a tour to some local sights so we took it – a bus ride around the island and up to a lookout where you could wonder at the curvature of the earth in all directions. Amazing! Then there was this little waterfall and swimming hole with the most gorgeous turquois water, that looked so inviting. The local kids who had come on the tour all jumped in for a swim. I didn't think to bring a bikini so I just enjoyed a seat in the shade watching and chatting with the other three tourist couples.

We were back at the hut in time to meet Clark and Dirk coming ashore after spending the day searching with the sonar and finding quite a few regular shaped distortions on the seabed that warranted further investigation tomorrow.

"Yes a good first day," Clark enthused. "Damn I'm hungry though."

"Yeah I could eat," Dirk agreed, slapping a hand on Linus's shoulder and we all strolled along the pier towards a café with a good dinner menu, we'd noted when investigating options this morning.

I was outnumbered by men and I liked it. I sat there watching them eat and drink and laugh. I'm hardly any more capable of doing or saying anything when men look at me than I am when they touch me. By the time my husband said goodnight to the other two men and took me to our hut, I was completely for the taking.

Clark showered and pulled me to him on a love seat looking out at the moonlit ocean, the night still and balmy. We could hear the gentle strum of a guitar in one of the other huts and some lovely native ballad singing.

"So I might see if Linus will take me back to that swimming hole tomorrow," I told my husband. "He said he can ride a scooter, so we could go on that."

"Oh yeah, so what's happening with Victoria, when is she back?"

"Tomorrow night, I think. It depends on what's happening with her thing. It sounded like she was thinking about flying back home to deal with it, not just to Tonga for better communications. Linus wasn't sure."

"Oh right." Clark chuckled. "That won't be good news for Dirk."

"Oh?" I blushed at what my husband was suggesting. "So, has he said anything?"

"Yeah he said he's allowed to keep fucking her. Apparently Victoria has talked Linus into it, saying it's only going to be a one-off and she wants to fully experience it."

"Hmm I see." I took a breath, my skin tingling a bit. "So poor Linus then, huh?"

"Oh yeah?" I felt my husband swallow. "Do you think?"

"Yes, well he missed out claiming her back tonight, didn't he! He's probably over there doing it for himself right now."

"Yeah I suppose," Clark said, stroking my hair and kissing my head. "The poor guy, huh? I mean especially if Victoria has to fly home and leave him here alone. Unless he goes home too."

"No, he said he's not going home. He's enjoying the cruise and doing the cooking for us. He said if necessary he'll stay by himself, and that if Victoria has to go and sort out her fashion thing, she'll be too busy to miss him anyway."

"Right. Makes sense," Clark agreed and took a big breath. "And you want to go swimming with him tomorrow, do you? Just him and you in one of your little bikinis."

I blushed. "Um yes. Or if there's no kids around tomorrow I could go topless for him."

Clark swallowed. "Oh right." He kissed my head again. "And would you want to, baby?"

"Uh huh I think so. I already did it on the yacht, so he'll probably be hoping I do it again."

"Yeah and would you let him do your sunscreen again too?" my husband asked, his cock flexing in his pants.

I squeezed it and looked up. "I'd definitely want him to, Clark. I can't wait for one of these other men to feel me up again."

"Right." My husband swallowed and took another big breath. "So we're going to do this then?" He stroked the hair from my face. "We're going to help him and Santos out with this while we're out here in the middle of the ocean with no women for them."

"Uh huh," I breathed into a kiss. "I've been thinking about it and I'd like to let them. Just in my mouth."

"Yeah, just in your mouth," my husband echoed, thumbing my lower lip and looking at my mouth. "I wonder if I should tell him again, he knows that's as much as we want to happen, doesn't he?"

"Hmm I'm sure he knows, Clark. You said that perfectly clearly the other night when we were talking about it."

"Yes and you'd actually do something if he tried to go further, wouldn't you baby? You'd be able to say no, wouldn't you?"

My blush fired up. "Um I think so. I'm not safe from getting pregnant, so I'm sure I'd be able to say stop if he was trying to have full on sex with me."

"Oh fuck," my husband groaned into my mouth, and he lifted me and carried me to the bed, dropping me on it.

I scooted back. He reached under my skirt and stripped my panties down and off my feet. I held the pillow above my head and relaxed as he positioned my legs bent up and apart. He stared at my pussy whilst stripping his clothing. He got a condom from his shaving bag and I couldn't help smiling but I bit down and held my breath as he got on top of me, positioned his cockhead and thrust into me. "Ahh huh huh," I moaned but bit down on that too.

My husband pulled me down the bed so I was flat on my back. Then he covered me and fucked me into a delicious orgasm. After holding himself back he finally powered into me to hold firm and ejaculate into his condom.

He pulled out and left me lying there with my legs still flopped wide open. He went and made coffees and took them back out onto the veranda. I used my panties to wipe my pussy, put them in my dirty wash bag and went out to join him.

"Maybe take some of my condoms with you tomorrow just in case?" Clark suggested.

I sipped my coffee. "Ah, okay…"

*

The next morning I wore a short skirt and bikini bottoms, with just one of my little see-through tube tops. Linus had eyes all over me from the moment he opened his door until we were at the scooter hire place. Then he made me drive and sat behind with his hands on my waist and me willing them to creep upwards, all the way to the swimming hole.

There was no one there. Yesterday it had only been our tour group, so we figured it would just be us until about 2 in the afternoon again.

"Are we going in for a swim today?" Linus asked.

We were standing on the sandy shore, dipping our toes. The water was lukewarm.

"I didn't bring a bikini top," I said.

The older man nodded, looked up from my tight nipples.

"You could swim in that."

I grimaced a bit and chewed my lip.

Linus looked around, shrugged. "It's only me here to see."

"Uh huh." I took a breath and expelled. "Would you rather I just took it off?"

"Yes." The older man looked down and up from my nipples again. "Yes I would."

I blushed. "Okay." I motioned to where we'd left our things next to the scooter. "I'll just um…"

I walked over and took my towel from my bag and laid it out on the sand. I then lowered to my knees and lifted my top off, showing the man my tits.

He laid out his towel and stripped his shirt and shorts then sat down with me. I was facing him, still on my knees, with my arms down straight and my chest up and forward.

"It's up to you if you're going to touch me or do anything, Linus. I'm more comfortable when the man's in charge unless it's a game and he's told me I can pretend to be."

Linus nodded, his eyes intense. He crawled forward and surprised me by taking hold of the back of my neck and kissing me.

I tensed up at first but quickly responded and relaxed in his hold. I opened my mouth and let him stick his tongue in as he worked me onto my back on the towel.

I had slumped with my legs bent up and to one side, both arms by my sides and my hands upturned in the sand. The older man was ravaging my mouth. His tongue probed deep to lash mine as he continued to hold the back of my neck with one hand and feel my tits with his other.

My mind was whooshing, like it always does. It was out of my body and up there watching what this new man was doing with me. "Ooh yeah this is so sexy, just lie there for me love," he groaned into my mouth. "Completely submissive yeah... I can do what I want?"

He had looked into my eyes, allowing me to focus enough to say, "But I'm not on birth control okay?" I swallowed. "Maybe just in my mouth, like with your tongue just then?"

"Oh yeah, I can fuck your mouth, can I love?"

I swallowed again, nodded. "You don't have to ask to do that. Whenever you need to while we're here and Victoria's away."

"Ah I see." Linus lifted to his knees and shuffled forward. He had kept hold of the back of my neck and held my head up whilst pulling the leg of his swimmers over his cock and freeing it to stick in my mouth.

I used my lips to protect it from my teeth but otherwise just relaxed my shoulders and arms and let him do this. He was snarling down at me, watching intently as his cock plunged in and out of my mouth. He settled into a steady rhythm and looked down my body, massaging from one of my tits to the other.

I just waited. This was exactly how it always happened with my husband. Fortunately Linus wasn't trying to stick his cock too far into my throat. It was going in a little bit but he wasn't forcing it. He wasn't too huge either, so it was nice feeling his balls bumping against my chin.

I thought again about how hard it had been for the men out to sea for nearly two weeks without any privacy, and I wondered if Linus's balls were really full now – whether he was banked up much and it was going to be extra yucky in a minute when he came.

I guess I was a little nervous with a new man doing this to me, so I was thinking too much and not enjoying it as much as usual. Then suddenly Linus thrust and held firm, grunting as his cock started throbbing and spurts of warm cum lashed and filled the back of my throat.

"Oh yeah love, that's it. There's a good girl," he encouraged.

I came out of my trance and smiled up at him. *Well, I'm smiling as best I can with his dick still in my mouth haha.*

The first gulp of semen had my eyes watering. He was still softly throbbing and I needed to swallow again.

"Ooh yeah, drink it down love."

He took his cock from my mouth and I swallowed again at the strong taste of him.

"Is that good?"

I nodded and took a breath. "You can make me do that whenever you need to. If it's on the yacht, just take me into the bedroom or somewhere else private is all I ask. I'll just submit like that and let you each time." I swallowed at the strong taste again, grimacing a little. "Gooey man juice. Yuck!"

Linus smiled. "Ah not so nice huh?"

"Um no, but that doesn't matter, does it? It's not about it tasting nice. It's about you dominating me and enjoying that power, and making me swallow your yucky semen is the exciting bit for you men, right?"

"Oh yeah it's exciting alright, love."

"Hmm good. I'm glad you enjoyed it." I smiled cheekily. "But it works both ways – just so you know."

"Oh?"

I nodded. "Separately. That's important. It has to be a completely separate thing, when I force you. It's not about doing it for each other. It's about you taking what you want from me, and then some other time, me taking what I want from you."

"Ah I see. Intriguing! And what will you take from me, love? I can hardly wait to experience that."

I stood and smiled back over my shoulder on my way to soak in the pond. "I like the look of your beard. Hope it's going to be scratchy!"

Clark

The coordinates I had were sketchy. Actually they were in dispute, from different research sources. I had a twenty square nautical mile area to focus my search on. It was beyond a coral reef but still in relatively shallow water, the seabed ranging from 50 to 150 feet around the atoll.

Dirk was an experienced diver, as am I. He was in for a cut of anything of value we found and was working alongside me while we had young Santos at the helm, sailing the yacht in narrow search lanes north-south today. We were saving imagery of anything we found, any seemingly unusual sedimentary distortions. It was painstaking work but we had quite an intriguing map of images beginning to develop.

I'd been planning this adventure for over a year now, since being involved in the salvage mission of the French wreck around the other side of the atoll. I'd been involved in the mission to find that wreck but sent home immediately we'd established its location and dived to actually discover it.

I had broadened the research way back in the planning stages and become convinced this British ship was also wrecked in the area, although I was unable to convince the university or secure any funding.

I was here now though and so excited to be glued to this antiquated little sonar screen trying to decipher the grainy images. I was also worried about my wife over on the island with Linus. I hoped he wouldn't fuck her.

I had discovered Leonie's penchant for submission early on. From our very first kiss, I'd noticed her relaxing into my hold on her – the way she offered zero resistance to being touched and felt. The first time I tried for a feel of her tits, she just relaxed her arm away and thrust one side of her chest forward. It had been in a movie theatre and she sat there throughout the film letting me do whatever I wanted with her body, including getting fingers into her pussy through the edge of her panties.

Of course, I was already intrigued by risky public sex, and we'd even discussed the idea. It was still fascinating and extremely arousing to feel the way Leonie submitted to being touched like that. It was something that came naturally to her and is the way she always is to this day.

So yeah, I was a bit worried about her being alone with Linus today. She was going to be encouraging him by sunbathing topless again. She was willing to suck him off. I wanted that to happen but could only hope Linus didn't take more.

I couldn't imagine Leonie actually resisting or denying whatever a man wanted from her. I adjusted my erection to one side in my pants and checked that Dirk up on deck monitoring and adjusting the side-sonar depth wasn't looking.

I seriously wanted this though. I had thought about it and decided Linus was an ideal candidate for allowing to be the first other man to experience my wife – the way she submits and lets you take her. I'd fantasised about this ever since I met her but had never been game to try it at home. It was definitely the vastness of the ocean and remoteness of our location that changed things. This would be something we tried whilst far away from home surrounded by nature.

It had my heart heavy in my chest but my balls tingled and my cock stayed semi-firm all day hoping that Linus was enjoying my wife. Hoping that he was looking at her bare tits and touching them, and that he got his cock in her mouth at some point and got her to swallow his cum.

"Alright, we swing around and do some east-west runs before we call it a day?" Dirk called down to me in the lower bridge.

"Uh yeah." I cleared my throat, shifted in my seat to hide my full boner. "Yeah, I'd like to keep at it until near dark. Try and get at least half of the area mapped lat' and long'. I want to be diving our first site by midday tomorrow. What do you think?"

Dirk slapped a powerful hand on my shoulder as he edged behind and past me. He smiled. "I say we can have a beer or three while we're at it since we've got the young bloke at the helm."

He handed me a beer on his way back past. We stuck at it, turning east-west and sailing narrow latitudinal search lanes, storing images and enhancing our map, which was quickly filling in with potential dive sites.

We anchored at dusk and took the runabout ashore. I left Dirk and Santos to their evening and went to find my wife. She was at our bungalow, lying in a hammock reading. She smiled a greeting and I bent to her and took her lips softly. They were warm and her breath was thick with a familiar scent. Tingles shot up my back and heated my neck and face as Leonie held me down and insisted on a deeper kiss.

I swallowed at the taste of her tongue. "Is that um..?"

My wife nodded, biting her lip and smile now. "Linus only just left. We saw you men come ashore and he went back to his bungalow but I decided to let you taste where he'd been instead of just saying."

"Right."

I let my wife pull me down into another kiss while she guided my hand between her legs. The musky taste of her mouth filled my senses as my fingers slipped into her heat and wetness. I immediately boned up and took over kissing her deeply and passionately whilst banging her with two fingers, both heels of her bare feet wedged between the cheeks of her arse, her legs bent up and spread wide.

"Did he fuck you?"

"Uh uh, I sat on his face and fucked myself on his beard. Then I kept him pinned down and sucked him off. Like five minutes ago. While you were walking up here from the jetty. He literally just walked around that corner when you walked around that one."

"Oh hell baby, so fucking sexy. I'm gonna nail you so fucking hard tonight."

"Mmm promise?"

"Yeah I promise, you dirty little slut." I stroked her hair from her sweaty face. "You taste like cum. Same as you do after me."

"Uh huh I know. I had a huge drink this morning that was even stronger than this one. But Linus said he'd been saving it for Victoria last night and that he doesn't enjoy masturbating, so he still hadn't."

"Oh right. Yeah I'm with him on that. No comparison," I said into another kiss.

"Plus I told him he can take me like that again when he needs to, Clark. And Victoria flew home today, so he's going to be here on his own for our whole stay and voyage home. They've agreed that she won't come back and that he should continue on without her."

"Oh right." I still had fingers up my wife, feeling into her for my own pleasure. "That's good then baby. We'll definitely let Linus cum in your mouth when he needs to, and maybe think about Santos and Dirk as well?"

"Mmm maybe. Uhh huh huh," my wife moaned and tensed, her cunt clenching around my fingers. "Uh huh huh I know I want to let Santos and maybe Dirk too," she uttered breathily, her body spasming on my fingers, her bare belly clenching with each contraction and her tits jiggling.

I had bared her tits, pushed her tube top up over them. I sucked a nipple, withdrawing my fingers and smoothing her cunt closed.

After a meal we had delivered from one of the café's, I took my ragdoll wife to bed and fucked her missionary, pulling out and ripping off the condom to cum all over her tits, then pulling her pyjama top back down and making her sleep in it.

"I want to come with you tomorrow, okay? I'll help Santos steer the boat while you and Dirk are diving."

"Oh yeah – help the boy drive the boat, will you?"

"Uh huh. Is that okay?" my wife teased sweetly over her shoulder, wriggling back against me down below. "I'm not sure how submissive I can be for him though. It only works with you men."

*

I awoke at dawn the next morning and left my wife sleeping while I had the local cab driver run me around the island to where the university crew were set up in their camp. They had the one huge ex-military tent for their sleeping quarters. The dive team were all men. There was a female Research Fellow working on the search earlier, but she was sent home with me. Otherwise there was the lab set up in Tonga and anything salvaged was being transported there for analysis and shipped home for further study.

It struck me funny to see a dozen men stuck all the way out here in a camp for weeks at a time without their wives or girlfriends. There were only the wives and young children of the fishermen on the island too. It seemed anyone of age had gone to high school on the mainland, never to return.

I found Professor Norris at breakfast in their mess tent. He welcomed me to grab a plate and join him. We got along okay. He was a bit of a dick, with his superiority complex going on, but we got along okay professionally.

I had brought printouts of the mapping we'd done so far. We had completed the full latitudinal search yesterday and had 57 identified sites to explore further.

"That's going to take a month," Norris warned, shaking his head. "You need to narrow it down somehow. Can you do a diagonal sweep, a third or even forth angle on those images could help."

"Yeah true." I drew and huffed a breath. "But then again with the limited resolution, there's no guarantee we haven't missed the actual wreck. So quite possibly another day mapping and still 50 dive sites that may amount to nothing."

Norris nodded, holding my gaze. He knew what I was doing here – what I was asking for.

I hoped that showing him what I was up against with sub-standard equipment might persuade him to help out. I even glanced suggestively at the sonar and computer equipment he had packed neatly away in its case and packing crate right there in the open storage container beside the mess tent.

He chuckled, shaking his head some more. "Man, I'd like to, but I can't."

I'd used the university's equipment before and knew its capabilities of course. "It would take one day and we could narrow down to five or ten sites... I know the wreck of the Sunline is there, Pete!"

"Well maybe so, but your application was refused, Clark. That wasn't my call, and I'm responsible for the recovery and all equipment here. I'd be taking a risk allowing you to take the sonar out to sea, entirely against directives." The guy shrugged. "It wouldn't even be casual misuse of equipment, without asking. You actually asked and were told you couldn't have it."

"Yeah right." I huffed and shook my head. The guy was right. I held up a hand. "Sorry man, I had to ask at least."

"Hey I get it. I would too buddy." Norris sipped his coffee. "So how's the trip going anyway? How's Leonie handling it?"

"Oh yeah good." I felt my face flush a little. "Yeah she's having a ball. Loves sailing and if we can score some more of these nice sunny days..!"

"Yeah, it's looking nice today," Norris agreed. "Forecast is for clear skies for the next week or so." He rocked back in his chair, folded his huge arms. "Tell Leonie to come visit herself if you like. I'd be happy to show her around the site here. We've got the new submersible drone working now, can show her around the wreck if she likes."

"Oh yeah?" I met my workplace superior's even gaze.

"And you too of course, Clark. If you have time one day."

I nodded, swallowed hard. "Yeah I guess Leonie's got plenty of time to kill. I'll let her know to come see you," I agreed.

What the fuck is this? Is he actually asking for this? Suggesting..!

I held the guy's gaze and saw the dare twinkling in it.

I nodded slowly, glancing back and forth to the sonar again.

"It would be a hell of a risk for me, Clark. Even to explain how you found anything so quickly without using that. The VC would figure it out in a heartbeat. He'll know if I let you use it, so there'd be consequences for me."

"Right. It'd cost you," I agreed, still trying to fathom the guys thinking and what he was playing at here.

He smirked then nodded. "Everything comes at a cost." He shrugged. "You have to be prepared to pay it is all."

He stood and walked past me, slapping a hand on my shoulder. "Tell Leonie I said hi, okay? Good luck diving today!"

I finished my coffee, said a quick hello to some of the crew and they showed me film from the new submersible drone. It was brilliant, the ocean crystal clear around the atoll, which was all good for diving. I had a drone too of course, but again a less sophisticated one than the university could afford, and I wasn't planning to use it unless the seafloor depth was more than a hundred feet. It was going to be quicker and more thorough to simply dive and dig around where possible.

I got back to the bungalow to find Leonie ready. We were a bit late actually and Dirk and Santos were waiting at the runabout.

"Sorry guys, I got held up with the university crew."

"That's alright. Are you coming with us today?" Dirk asked, smiling broadly at Leonie.

"Yes, Linus was so tired after our adventure yesterday and needs a rest, so you're stuck with me today, I'm afraid."

"Haha you wore the poor old bugger out did you?"

Dirk was helping Leonie down into the runabout. It was below the level of the pier. She climbed backwards down the ladder with Santos tilting his head from the stern of the little boat to look up her skirt. Leonie had on panties, not bikini bottoms, so the boy was getting a good view.

When she sat there was a flash of white between her thighs too, with Dirk getting a look that time.

Leonie's skirt was short and straight. She knelt on her seat and reached to pull in the rope Dirk had tossed onto the bow. She had to reach for it and I met a glance from Dirk as he had a look up the back of her skirt at her panty covered crotch and bare arse cheeks with the G-string between them. He winked at me. "Nice."

I nodded and looked at Santos too. "Sounds like we've lost Victoria, so it's just Leonie now."

She turned around and sat, blushing at us. Her tits were barely concealed beneath a short tank top, her nipples poking at it as usual.

"So just you to keep us guys company now, huh?" Dirk said.

"Uh huh, I'll try," Leonie answered sweetly. "It's easier for me, with all you men. It must be hard for you guys in that way."

"Yeah it can be. You're certainly a sight for sore eyes though," Dirk went on as Santos took us away from the pier and swept around to head out towards the reef and where the yacht was anchored.

The outboard was too loud to talk over but I liked that short exchange. It had been a good start in letting these guys know Leonie was here for all of us men and not just for me. We were sitting facing the guys at the back and they were both looking up Leonie's skirt and at her tits. I just massaged the back of her neck and could feel her excitement in the way her nails were digging into my thigh.

When we got to the yacht, I climbed up first and helped Leonie. Dirk and Santos grinned to each other and shared a look up her skirt from behind again.

"Ooh yeah nice!" Dirk called out and made her blush back down at him. "Very nice!"

"Hmm well I'm pleased you think so," she shot back, glaring playfully. "I suppose I should have worn shorts today."

"Hell no, that's a cute little skirt," Dirk told her. "It's a good view up it." He winked to me again as he tilted for another look while Leonie faced him and raked back her hair in the breeze.

I squeezed her shoulders and had her snuggling back against me. "You guys go ahead and enjoy," I called down to them lifting supplies from the runabout. "Leonie doesn't mind you looking, do you baby?"

"No I don't mind. I feel flattered that you'd both want to."

"Fuck yeah, we want to, eh Santos?" Dirk encouraged.

Santos gulped. "Hell yeah!"

I left my wife with the guys and went to get organised with my laptop and map. I heard a shriek and giggle then saw Leonie lunge away from Dirk but he caught her again and had her cuddled to his front whilst starting the boat and hitting the anchor winch. He kept her with him whilst heading us out into open water. He let her have a drive and just held her hips.

I was peeping from down below and saw Leonie's arms lift away from her sides as Dirk rubbed upward. Her hand rested upon his wrist as he cupped a tit and squeezed then thumbed the nipple, rubbing it as she steered the boat.

Dirk took over steering but kept my wife cuddled in front of him, casually playing with her tits and nipples. I could see directly up the back of her skirt and between her thighs. I could see how damp the crotch of her panties was and how it was pasted to her cunt and creased into it.

133

I took my list of coordinates up the stairs, clearing my throat before popping my head up. Dirk released Leonie and left her steering on her own. I gave him the list. He entered the first of them into the GPS and took back over steering to get us there.

Leonie grimaced guiltily as she headed along to the main stairs and down to the lower deck lounge and her bedroom. I stayed at the bridge with Dirk, watching the marker on the GPS screen, we would be there in a few minutes but already had our diving gear ready yesterday. Santos took over at the helm and Dirk and I headed down to the bow ramp and got suited up. Once we'd reached the coordinates and Santos cut the main engines and engaged the GPS auto positioning, Dirk and I dropped into the water and dived down the 50 feet to what had looked a quite promising sediment formation on our grainy sonar screen.

We found it right away but digging in the sand we only found rock beneath, part of a ridge of rock protruding in a long shelf.

We concluded immediately and shook heads at each other then headed back to the surface.

Leonie

I kept out of the way and read a book on my eReader while the men hopped from one dive site to the next all morning. Sometimes they would just hold the boat with the motors and do a quick dive, then drop the anchor and go back down for a better look.

They had tried five different sites before breaking for the lunch I had prepared for them. Then into the afternoon, I stayed with Santos and helped do the steering. We had anchored at another site and Dirk and Clark had gone back for a second look around.

"Hey you!" I scolded Santos grabbing and tickling my ribs.

We had nothing to do but wait. He was looking naughty and playful. I was getting tingles and wanting to submit to him as he held my hips from behind but I shrieked and jumped again when he gripped and tickled.

I ran and he chased me downstairs. I was squealing and he was jumping couches and lunging for me. He tackled me onto a couch and was on top of me, one leg between mine. I squirmed and thrashed about. He got a hand up my top and squeezed my tit. A surge of tingles nearly made me give in, but I pretended to relax and when he relaxed too I jumped clear of his clutches and ran shrieking up the stairs to the men resurfacing.

"How did it go?" I asked as they climbed aboard.

"Nothing but rock again," Clark said frustratingly.

I watched them pull their wetsuits down to the waists, enjoying another look at Dirk's amazing body. He was repaying the compliment by looking directly up my skirt. "Ooh that's nice," he groaned but I just glared defiantly and turned away.

Santos was back at the bridge raising the anchor. He grinned cheekily at me as I approached.

"No more tickling you!" I scolded, taking over the wheel as we headed off to our next beep on the GPS screen.

It was only a five-minute run and the guys were pulling up their suits again. Santos held the yacht in position with the engines. Dirk did the initial dive. They were taking turns and both going down if there was anything worth exploring. He was back pretty quickly and we sailed to the next marker on the map where Clark dived and found nothing. Then we sailed to the next dive site and Dirk came back up saying there was a long ridge of sediment they needed to check more thoroughly.

We dropped anchor and Clark and Dirk dived in. I was watching them as far as I could see in the clear water. I was leaning right over and Santos grabbed me from behind and tickled again.

I squirmed away from him and ran shrieking with laughter as he chased me. I ran downstairs and he tackled me onto a couch again. He was clutching my ribs and making me laugh hysterically, but this time when he stopped tickling, he kissed me, pressing his lips against mine and demanding I kiss him back.

He had shocked me a little and I submitted to him forcing his tongue into my mouth. I relaxed under the young guy and moved my arm out of the way when he started feeling my breasts. He suddenly stopped kissing me and sucked one of my nipples, latching onto it and suckling while I watched and just lay there with my arms draped aside and my top now up to my neck.

"Aw fuck these are amazing Leonie. You've got great tits," the guy said, eyes wide as he peered up at me.

I just breathed and swallowed, nodding a little.

The young man resumed sucking from one nipple to the other. I hadn't fully submitted to him but he was making me tingle between the legs and I didn't know what I was going to do if he tried to touch me down there.

A call came over the radio. It was the local authorities requesting contact. Santos rushed off to get the call and I lay there taking some calming breaths and fixing my clothing.

The local coast guard was passing on warnings about storm activity heading our way, also checking on our plans for the next few nights regarding where we would be anchoring and giving details of course plans for some cruise ships passing by.

I waited for the guys to resurface and helped them up and with their gear. There had been wreckage this time but it was a rusted metal hull of something that must have sunk about thirty years ago and had been fully salvaged of anything worthwhile already.

Dirk went and saw Santos about the call from the coast guard. I made coffees for the men and took them a slice of cake I had baked them this morning. After a short afternoon break we checked another three sites and dropped anchor at a fourth.

As soon as the two mature men were gone, the young cheeky one was at me again. He looked more serious now and I just pushed away from him and kept him at arm's length as I backed down the stairs. He grabbed me and carried me back onto a couch. He landed on top of me with his mouth over mine, his tongue demanding entry again.

I opened and accepted his kiss. He pulled my top up but barely felt my tits before rubbing down my belly and feeling between my legs. He rubbed into me and stretched the crotch of my soggy panties aside. "Uh huh huh," I moaned as his fingers entered me.

I squeezed my thighs together but tingles were surging all through me and I couldn't help submitting to the guy. I relaxed my legs and mouth open and he ravished me with his tongue and fingers.

"Um Santos!" I uttered but couldn't do much else as he urgently pushed at his board shorts.

He was suddenly thrusting between my legs and my eyes shot open when he entered me like that. "Uh huh huh," I moaned and gripped his narrow hips, pushing against them with all the resistance I could muster. "Um no Santos," I said but he was crushing me into the couch and spearing into me, humping urgently.

"Santos no!" I cried and reached down between us. He was quite small but so hard as he plunged in and out of me. I got my hand around his penis and squirmed away from his next thrust.

"Aw fuck," he complained.

He had stopped thrusting and I slithered down beneath him and took him into my mouth. "Nya fuck yeah," he groaned approvingly now and I kept hold of his shaft and bobbed on the head, sucking and lashing with my tongue. "Nya fuck!" he cried out and I stopped bobbing and held the head of his cock in, releasing the shaft and allowing him to plunge deep into my mouth as he ejaculated.

"Mmm hmm," I hummed and held and squeezed his little butt. It was another huge drink I was getting. The young man arched above me, gripping the back of the couch and kneeling on the seat with one knee. I was sitting on the floor, my head all the way back, his smooth young balls resting on my chin and gently pulsating as they emptied.

I did a second big swallow then let his spent cock dangle. I nuzzled his balls and kissed from one to the other then sucked his cock back into my mouth and swirled it around with my tongue, making sure to suck the last dribbles of semen out of it, smiling at the way it made him convulse in obvious pleasure.

"Hmm you can't have me fully. I'm not on birth control," I scolded, squeezing his cock to one side and glaring up at him smiling down at me.

"Sorry I couldn't help it."

"Yes I know, but you have to help it. I need you to care for me if I'm going to be doing this for you, Santos. It's hard for me to even think when you touch me, so I need you to control yourself and not go too far with me."

141

"Oh right. So just finger you and that?"

"Um I don't know. If you want to do that you can, but you can't have full sex with me."

The young guy gulped and nodded. "Okay, so not actually fuck you but other stuff's alright. And then you'll suck me off again?"

I felt myself blush a little. I nodded, biting my lip. "Or you can just do it with my mouth. I don't mind if a man wants to hold my head and pretend he's having me like that. As long as you don't try to go too deep in my throat."

"Oh right, so to fuck your mouth then?"

"Hmm yes, if you want to be crude and say it like that."

The guy chuckled. "And all the way till I shoot my load, huh?"

I blushed deeper and rolled my eyes. "Yes but again, not too deep please. Especially when you're cumming. I'd rather you pulled back a bit and just did that in my mouth instead of all the way down my throat." I was sitting up on the couch now, tugging my top into place. "I'm willing to swallow your cum, but I'd like to do it nicely and not have to choke on it, okay?"

"Ah yeah. Okay. Cool," the young guy enthused. "I'd better um..!" He motioned to top deck, where he was supposed to be watching for the men diving.

I went and flopped on my bed. I was pleased to have done that for Santos. It had been a big load, although at his age it may well have only been from that day. I imagined he would be giving me lots of big loads to swallow, and I smiled to myself at the thought of asking him not to do it himself and to save it all for me to drink.

I heard the men and soon enough we were sailing again. Then we stopped and all was quiet for another little while before I heard Clark complaining about another worthless piece of wreckage, just a length of metal pipe.

I dozed off and woke to the rocking of the boat and lashing of rain against the windows. We were back at the island and anchored for the night. I pulled on a raincoat and got drenched on the trip ashore in the open runabout.

We showered and had a meal delivered. Dirk, Santos and Linus joined us and we had an impromptu party with a few bottles of wine for me and Linus. The other men drank bourbons. It had turned cold with the storm, and I stayed wrapped in a jumper with long pants and woolly socks on. I still liked the way all these men were looking at me and obviously thinking about me beneath the clothing.

Nothing came of the night though, everyone got rather drunk then all the men stumbled back to their own bungalows to sleep it off.

I hadn't even had a chance to tell my husband I'd sucked off our eager young deckhand yet, but I went to sleep remembering how hard he had been in my mouth and hoped he'd be excited for that to happen again tomorrow. I was so thirsty for more semen from these men now. I loved the idea of doing it for all of them, and anytime any of them needed it.

Mmm yummy – like a nice warm drink of milk. Extra creamy! Oh god I've had fantasies about drinking from even more men than this, especially watching the guys playing footy at the oval next to our house. The local men's team trains there three nights a week and I often watch and dream about being taken into their change room when they're showering. I wouldn't mind how many of them wanted to have their turn in my mouth.

144

*

"Morning baby, how are you feeling?" my husband asked.

I yawned and stretched. "Never better. How about you?"

"Yeah good. Fit and ready, but I don't know how we're going to go with this. There's too many sites to check and this glorified fish-finder we've used could well have missed the wreck we're looking for completely if the hull is angled wrong. Everything we've dived to so far is either north-south or east-west. It's all ridges of rock or sea junk lying either predominantly one way or the other. I don't think we'll find the Sunline unless it happens to be positioned directly across the path of our search lanes."

I squeezed my husband's hand in my lap. We were sitting up in bed. It was breaking dawn on the ocean horizon through our open bungalow doors. He'd brought us coffees.

Clark took a big breath and expelled. "I've got to try and get the uni sonar from Norris again. We're wasting our time."

"Okay. So will he give it to you?"

"Huh! Not for free."

"Oh. He wants to be paid for it? When it's not even his to hire out?"

"Yeah well, it's as good as his right now, baby. I'm going to have to see what he wants for it. He hinted that everything has a price." Clark glanced at me. "I can't imagine any amount of money would sway him. He's fucking loaded, isn't he!"

"Uh huh, he seems to be." I looked at my husband. "Would you like me to ask him?"

Clark didn't remove his gaze from the sunrise, his jaw set.

"I wouldn't mind if you wanted me to," I went on, squeezing his hand with both of mine. "You know what he's like. He might respond better to a woman."

Clark swallowed hard. "Huh! Yeah…"

My blush fired up. "Which I wouldn't mind playing up to if it suited us."

My husband took another big breath and expelled. He swallowed hard again and looked at me, glancing down and back up from my bare tits, the bedclothes at my waist. I had slept nude.

He nodded. "I guess he's a bit of a dick, but he's not so bad. Not a lot different from the likes of Dirk obviously enjoying the fact you're female."

My blush intensified and tingles surged through my body. "Hmm I'm definitely female for Dirk, and for the other two men we're sailing with."

"Yeah true," my husband agreed and cupped my face, kissing me softly. "Especially for Linus the other day."

I smiled into our kiss. "Hmm and for Santos yesterday when you were diving one time."

"Oh right, so..?"

"Uh huh, he got too frisky and I had to suck him off."

"Oh okay. Good then." Clark nodded. I saw the sheet move, tenting in his lap a little as he reached for his coffee and had a sip. "Okay so you've done it for Linus and Santos now. That's good baby. That's fucking hot to think about."

"Mmm apparently," I said and squeezed the tent. "Ooh that's um…"

147

"Yeah that's been happening a lot since we started doing this baby, but it's more about the idea of you going to see Norris right now. I think I'd already decided I was going to ask you to but I'm just worried he might fuck you if you go on your own."

Hot tingles flushed through my entire body again. I couldn't say anything in response to that. It was up to my husband to decide and tell me to go or not.

He held me close and kissed the top of my head. "I know he'll expect to be allowed to fuck you if he gives us the sonar, baby... I don't think there's any doubt about that," my husband groaned and his cock flexed powerfully in my fist as I squeezed and just about went into orgasm myself right then and there.

***

Part 4: Female Company for the Crew

Leonie

"Okay, I say we go and see Norris this morning. There's no point wasting more time with all these dive sites. We need that high-tech sonar and software. We're just going to have to ask him again and be prepared to go along with what he wants, if you really think you could do that baby?"

My husband was asking but to me it was a command. I snuggled against his chest.

"I doubt he'd try anything this morning. Not if I don't let him take you anywhere alone." He kissed my head. "He's definitely going to know I've given in to him though. We were both looking at the sonar in its packaging crate and he said everything has its price and that I should send you to see him."

"Hmm, he said that straight out?"

"Yeah." My husband stroked and kissed my hair again. "And he's clearly always had it bad for you at work, right?

I mean there's no doubt he's always wanted to get onto you, baby."

"Uh huh I know. He's really obvious about it, Clark. He'll be so proud of himself if we do this – getting the better of you and having his way with me."

Clark gulped. "Yeah, and he'll definitely want to fuck you. He wouldn't be satisfied with anything else."

"Mmm do you think?" I asked, masking my excitement.

"Yeah baby, and I wouldn't expect you to try and deny him or anything. He wouldn't be like young Santos. Norris is a grown man."

I swallowed and my skin tingled all over.

"But it's not much different to what's happened with Santos and Linus so far," my husband went on, trying to convince himself by the sound of it. "It's no different to what's probably going to happen with Dirk too if we let him touch you. I can't see him being satisfied with less than full sex either, baby."

I held my husband's erection through the sheet. I thumbed over the head and a wet spot formed. It was getting lighter outside. The morning sun peeped over the ocean horizon through our bungalow window now. I peered up, grimacing guiltily at how excited this was making me too.

Clark met my lips. "Which is obviously a problem unless they agreed to use condoms with you, huh?"

"Um I was thinking about that. I think I might be late enough in my cycle. I should be past ovulation by now."

"Oh right! Do you think?"

I lifted and straddled my husband's lap, freeing his erection from the fly of his boxers and sinking down onto it. He groaned and I squirmed on him, gyrating my hips and taking about a minute to get him to ejaculate. Then I immediately climbed off and rested beside him cuddled to his chest again.

"I'm sure that was safe," I told him.

"Aah fuck." He swallowed hard and huffed a couple of big breaths. "Right. Okay then. So if it came to it, we wouldn't have to worry about that at least."

"No and I don't see how I could ask either Professor Norris or Dirk to stop and put on a condom when, as soon as either of them touch me, I'm going to turn into a ragdoll like usual."

"Yeah true," my husband agreed, kissing my head again.

"Yes and I'd prefer them to have me fully, instead of just oral. Linus and Santos are both quite small and they were gentle when they were having my mouth. And Dirk looks really huge and I bet Professor Norris would be too, judging by the way he struts around campus. I'd much rather have them fuck me where their huge thingies are supposed to fit."

I felt my husband nodding. "Yep." He cleared his throat a little. "Makes sense, baby."

I giggled and felt my slippery pussy. "Oops." I was dripping. I lifted my fingers to show him then sucked them. My husband groaned approvingly.

Clark

It wasn't only Norris, it would be the whole salvage crew we'd be seeing at this hour of the morning. I had limited days to find the wreck of the HMS Sunline though and absolutely needed this equipment.

I hoped I'd be able to handle this. I wasn't certain, but it felt so surreal being all the way out here in the middle of the Pacific, on a tiny island inhabited by a couple of hundred local Polynesian people and staying only a few kilometres by taxi from the university's salvage site of the 1770 French explorer ship.

It had happened now. I felt okay with some of our crew having sex with my wife. Leonie and I had discussed it beforehand and allowed it to happen. There had been two other men enjoy my wife's mouth and she'd swallowed their cum. She was flashing and going topless for them and although our alpha captain Dirk hadn't had sex with her yet, he'd certainly felt her up a few times. It was only a matter of time.

I figured if I could handle her being played with by the other men on our boat, I'd be okay with my arrogant superior Professor Norris getting onto her.

Leonie was dressed in a short skirt that flashed her panties and a cheesecloth shirt open over a thin tube top, her nipples showing through both garments.

"Thank you." I paid the buxom lady taxi driver and she left us and drove to a parking space in front of the university camp office to pick up another fare.

Leonie kept her shirt wrapped around and her arms folded as we said hello to some of the all-male crew having breakfast. It seemed Norris was over in the office. The guys eating all tilted to look at Leonie's arse and legs as we walked away.

We approached the office and I peeped in the window to see Professor Norris on a laptop. He was alone in the small prefab humpy. I grabbed my wife's hand and pulled her back from going up the stairs.

I took a few breaths and decided this. "How about you go in and say hello, ask him to show you footage of their wreck from their submersible drone? I'll hang back here and say hello to these guys," I said as some of the salvage crew were just arriving ashore in a small runabout.

"Um okay," Leonie agreed, grimacing and taking off her shirt. She handed it to me and I scrunched it in my sweaty hands. "Does this look alright?"

"Aw fuck baby, you might as well be topless."

Leonie's nipples were erect and it must have been the thinnest of her little boob tops she had on. It was white and virtually see-through, cut off just below her tits and showing a boob bulge out the bottom. She tugged at it so it covered them but then smoothed the waistband of her skirt and pulled it up a bit until the crotch of her little G-string panties was almost showing.

"He can fuck me if he wants," my wife whispered. "I'll ask about us borrowing the sonar and just let him have me in exchange if he agrees to it."

I gulped hard. "Okay baby, tell him we'll have it back to him by tomorrow night." I stroked my wife's hair and kissed her salty lips. "Tell him you'll bring it back yourself, okay?"

My wife bit down on her smile. "Mmm okay, bad husband. I'll tell your boss he can fuck me now and that he can fuck me again tomorrow if he lends you his silly sonar," she teased and left me tilting for a view of her arse up the back of her skirt as she climbed the stairs and knocked.

"Hi Professor Norris!" she said sweetly.

"Leonie! Hey, come on in!" his deep voice resounded from the small office, and I ducked back around the corner of the wall as he appeared and ushered my wife inside with his arm going around her and his huge hand claiming her waist.

There were men I knew walking up from the runabout but I avoided them and snuck around the back of the office with my heart thumping in my throat.

I could only hear muffled voices from inside, some deep laughs and high-pitched ones. I was hanging close enough to intervene if it got to be too much and I changed my mind here. Norris was powerfully built and taller than me, but I could pull him off my wife if I had to.

The laughter ended, the voices still there but quieter. There was another window just around the corner of the back wall. There was a shipping container alongside the office and I edged between and peeped in the window.

Norris had my wife pressed back against a wall with her eyes glazed. He bent to her and kissed her. My heart sank but I was fascinated to watch. I hadn't really thought this through and wasn't prepared to see Leonie being kissed. The images I conjured up when thinking about it were of her sucking a cock or being fucked.

This surprised and intrigued me. I could see Leonie's arms were relaxed down by her sides. Norris felt up under her top and massaged her tit. I was watching from behind him but it looked like he had deepened the kiss. He suddenly broke off though and lowered to his knees in front of her, lifting her top and exposing both tits fully, then sucking on one of them.

Leonie remained resting back against the wall with her arms down, her head lowered to watch what the guy was doing but her eyes were glazed.

She had completely submitted. Whether she even asked for the sonar or not, she was Norris's for the taking. Whatever he wanted to do to her, he could.

He left both of her tits wet and reddened and guided her forward, bending her over his desk. It was now or never for me to stop this. Norris undid his shorts and pushed them down. He was bolt upright and fucking huge. He slapped Leonie's arse with his cock then slipped a finger beneath and stretched the string crotch of her little panties aside. He crouched with his cock in his fist and his head tilted to see where he was sticking the damned thing.

I couldn't watch any longer and turned away from the window, slumping back against the wall as I heard my wife cry out. She let out another squeal and I pressed my hands to my ears, muffling the sound of another and another squeal. I dared to sneak a peek again and saw my alpha boss thumping against my wife's butt, her bare tits bouncing on his desk.

He held her by the hips and thrust with his pelvis. From side-on I could see how he came a long way out of her before spearing back in and making her mouth gape. My heart was aching but I was mesmerised. The guy had my wife bouncing on his cock and her nipples rubbing on his desktop, papers were being pushed aside and skewing onto the floor.

Leonie was silent now and completely submissive, the way she always is. The guy behind her humped her until his face contorted and he thrust one final time and held firm, fully inside of her, his arse cheeks clenched and remaining so whilst he was no doubt emptying his balls.

He rested forward with one hand on the back of Leonie's neck and the other planted on the table. He was smirking down at her, pulling back and slowly thrusting forward to grind against her butt. The guy was enjoying an after-fuck of my wife now. He'd obviously pumped his load into her cunt and had it all slippery and hot. He still looked erect and so fucking huge, he must have been stretching her and enjoying how tight she was for him.

I couldn't blame the guy now. I know how it feels inside Leonie after you fuck her from behind. She keeps her hips tilted for you to enjoy her, just like she was doing right now.

I walked away from the office and sat under a nearby tree, watching the now-closed door. It was only a few minutes later the door opened and Norris came out still

159

doing up his pants. He saw me immediately and strolled over.

"Clark! How's things, man. Leonie says you had a slow day yesterday, things aren't workin' so well."

"Yeah that's right. I need to narrow down my search."

"Yes, so your wife was explaining. She's persuasive too, hey buddy. She's changed my mind about letting you use the equipment." The guy grinned smugly. "I'm sure you knew she would."

I swallowed and nodded stiffly. "So we can take it with us now, can't we?" I was looking beyond the guy to the open office door.

Norris looked back over his shoulder. "Ah she's just freshening up." He smirked. "Don't worry man, I know how to be discrete. No one back home will ever find out about this from me."

I nodded some more and took a breath. "Thanks," I said. I genuinely appreciated him saying that. He sounded sincere.

I was still sitting back against the tree. Norris knelt and glanced back at the office again before looking me in the eyes. "Your wife's a good fuck the way she just submits like that. You're a lucky man, Clark."

"Yeah thanks, I think so." My embarrassment had faded and my heart no longer felt heavy. The guy was being okay about this and I was okay with it too now. I actually liked what just happened and wanted to make sure of the deal. "So Leonie will bring the sonar back tomorrow and visit you again if you want, man?"

Norris nodded slowly and looked up from where he was fiddling with a stick. He shrugged. "I've got a better idea… I'd like to come along and bring the university's equipment with me – keep it in my possession since I'm the one it's signed out to. And that way I'm not technically handing it over."

"Oh right." I had to think quickly here. I couldn't see a problem with the idea. "Okay, so today? We've wasted too much time already."

"Yes today," Norris agreed. "Give me two hours to sort a few things here and I'll bring it with and meet you at your runabout."

"Right. Sure," I agreed too. "But it's probably going to take all day and part of tomorrow. We need to start again and map with the higher resolution imaging. I'm not confident we haven't passed right over the wreck and missed it."

"Hey that's fine. I'll hand over to the crew. I was going to be flying home this afternoon anyway. I won't be missed here."

"Oh shit. Brilliant!" I enthused. Norris was more skilled with using the software program than I was. Him being involved in our mapping would enhance the possibility of finding our wreck.

This was fantastic actually. "Can you bring scuba gear? Would you be willing to dive with us?" I asked hopefully.

Norris shrugged. "Course, happy to. As long as I get a mention if we find the Sunline."

"Hell yes. Of course! We're all in this. My captain is working as hard as I am. The owner of the boat only last night offered to finance an extended stay if we needed it and wants to be in on the salvage mission." I held my

Professor's steady gaze. "We're all partners in this, Pete. You're more than welcome to join in."

"Okay good. I'll take you up on that Clark. As long as we can have this equipment back in its box by tomorrow night, as you say."

"Absolutely!" Leonie had come from the office. I stood and brushed off my shorts and took Norris's hand and shook it as he stood too. "This is brilliant, Pete. I should have asked you to be involved from the start. It never occurred to me you'd be interested."

Norris looked at my wife with me. She was smiling over, not wanting to interrupt by the looks.

"Well I'm still not convinced the Sunline is here Clark, but er…" He motioned to my beautiful wife. "Like I said – persuasive!"

"Yeah…" I swallowed, feeling my face flush as I suddenly remembered what had just happened between Norris and my wife. A little surge of excitement welled up in me too though. "Yeah Leonie's happy to brighten things up for us all out at sea. Breaks up the all-male crew thing."

"Aah nice!" Norris enthused. "So she'll be sailing with us today and tomorrow?" He winked, grinning. "Keeping us entertained, yeah?"

I swallowed again, my face feeling cold now but I instantly wanted this. "Yeah I'm sure she won't mind if she has to persuade you some more, Pete... You're welcome to try and fuck her again while we're out there if you want."

"Damn straight I'm gonna want to. That was my first in over a week. Stuck out here with, like you said, an all-male crew."

I nodded and swallowed again. "Exactly! That's how Leonie sees it too and she wants to help out – make it better for all of us." I looked at the guy squarely again. "But discretely. Like you said. That would be much appreciated."

"Hell yes discretely! This is amazing Clark. It's hard to keep your eyes off her at work and it's more than how hot she looks. I've always seen something in her eyes and been intrigued."

"Yeah well, meet my wife, man. She's absolutely being herself with this but it's something she obviously can't take to work with her."

"Haha true that. True indeed." Norris glanced at me. "And that was alright, unprotected like that? I'm clean."

"Yeah no that's um." I gulped, nodded a bit. "We've talked about it and she says she should be safe from getting pregnant right now."

"Ah right. So all good to cum inside her then. Nice!"

"Yeah man, just cum in her. That's fine," I said and experienced a rush of excitement filling me at the thought.

"Haha," Norris chuckled, slapping a hand on my shoulder and giving me a powerful squeeze and shake then leaning close. "I certainly did that buddy. Haven't cum that hard in I don't know how long. Gave her a belly full, I can tell you."

I imagined how deep the guy's cock would have been in her when he was cumming and imagined Leonie's belly full of his cum right now as she questioned with another big smile over at us.

165

I left Norris to do what he needed and collected my wife. I took her to the taxi that was dropping off one of the university crew. We held hands and looked into each other's eyes, saying nothing on the way back to the village.

Santos was waiting at the pier with the runabout. I let him know we'd be another few hours and sent him to explain to Dirk we were getting the university sonar.

Leonie had gone to our bungalow. I found her in the bathroom rinsing her panties in the sink. I approached behind and squeezed her shoulders. "So Norris is sailing with us."

"Uh huh, he said he was going to ask if he could."

"Right." I kissed my wife's shoulder and cuddled her with my hands on her belly. "And you're sure you're safe from getting pregnant?"

"Hmm yes, and it's a bit late to worry about that now anyway."

"Yeah true. I was watching through the window back there. I saw him fuck you, baby."

"Uh huh, and did you like it?"

I swallowed. "Yeah I liked it." I sat across our small dining table and rested back, taking a big breath and expelling. "It's good that he's going to be helping with the search. It increases our chances significantly – him and the high-resolution capabilities of the sonar. His advice on sonar depths and widths of our search lanes, and deciphering the images – it's a huge bonus to have him join in."

"Yes and that's good, right?"

"Yeah it's good, and he's a half-decent kind of bloke when you get past how full of himself he is. I've always gotten on pretty well with him by not challenging too much, letting him have his say and not arguing unless it's absolutely necessary. Yep, as long as he thinks he's king shit."

"Hmm I know all about that, don't worry. From you telling me constantly about it after work regularly," Leonie smiled defiantly. "And you can go on bitching about his arrogance all you want after he's helped us find the wreck, can't you!"

"Yeah I guess." I swallowed and took another breath. "The only thing is that I told him he could try and fuck you again while we're out at sea. I don't know why I said it but I just did."

Leonie's blush fired up a bit, making her even prettier. "It's okay Clark, I don't mind that." She bit her lip and little smile. "I won't mind if any of you men need to take me into the bedroom while we're out at sea."

"Yeah?" My entire body flushed with nervous excitement. "You won't mind that there's so many of us?"

"Uh uh, I won't mind. You three strong men are going to be busy diving and searching for the wreck, and young Santos has to do all the driving and Linus will be cooking for us and making his awesome meals three times a day. I think it's only fair that I take care of you men in that way."

"Yeah right. All five of us! That's a lot, isn't it baby? It's not too many?"

"No that's fine. It's perfect," my wife uttered, slipping onto my lap now. "I can use my hand and my mouth. There's no limit to how much semen I can swallow Clark, and there's no limit to how much I can take like Professor

Norris gave his to me this morning." She kissed me and said into my mouth, "I can be the sex dolly they keep filling up as much as they all need to."

"Aw fuck," I groaned, my cock flexing in my thin board shorts and the head poking into my wife's hot and moist panty crotch, making her giggle as she wiggled on it.

Linus

The fresh produce on this island was amazing. I had young Santos helping me unload the taxi and pack the boxes up off the floor of the runabout, taking up some of the seating but leaving enough room for us and the lovely Leonie we could see strolling along the pier towards us.

Apparently she was coming with us while Clark waited for his Professor friend to arrive shortly.

"Morning beautiful!" I greeted the girl.

She was absolutely radiant, her long golden hair in the breeze, her tummy bare and a good view up a tiny crop top to the underside of her tits. Her long tanned legs and the firm little cheeks of her butt were bare and there was a flash of white lace between them as she turned to climb down the ladder.

I rolled my eyes at Santos. He was smiling his head off seated at the back of the boat with the outboard humming. I took my seat behind our young boat driver while Leonie raved about all the fantastic looking fresh fruit and vegies.

Once we were headed out to the reef and the yacht anchored beyond, she rested back on her hands with her head rocked back as she basked in the lovely morning sun.

The girl kept her knees together but there was an even better view up her crop top now. Her nipples were erect and the thin white fabric was peaked over them, her small dark areola visible poking out underneath.

I was staring, so was Santos. She looked at us and giggled knowingly, rolling her eyes and lifting her top up higher to expose her tits fully.

"Better?" she challenged us.

I shifted a box and sat beside her. I took out my sunscreen and squirted a blob into my hand. She bit down on her smile as I rubbed it into her tits. "You need to be careful love, you don't want to burn."

170

"Uh huh thank you," she uttered and arched upward as I continued massaging and playing with her nipples now.

I tweaked one then the other. She held her top up out of the way. She bit her lip and watched what I was doing. I tilted in and kissed her, cupping the back of her neck and moving over her to deepen and lash her tongue, her arms draped by her sides, her body limp and her eyes glazed.

I lifted from the girl and checked on our young driver. He was reaching out his foot and pressed against the inside of her knee and moved her leg aside. "Oh love," I groaned into her hair, continuing to feel her tits. I resumed kissing her as the young guy pressed his foot against her other knee and parted that leg as well.

The girl remained slumped back in her seat with her legs open a ways but not really spread, just relaxed apart and showing the crotch of her little panties quite nicely now.

I sat back and left her with her mouth wet and open and her tits in the sun. She smiled from me to Santos and back, her pretty eyes telling us to take her as we pleased. We were soon at the yacht though and kept busy carting my fresh produce up and down into the galley. Dirk was helping but continually looked to see where Leonie had gone, which was into the main sleeping berth.

Santos returned to shore in the runabout. I was busy organising my kitchen and preparing for what I was planning to cook over the next few days. I could hear Leonie and Dirk in the lounge area chatting but it got quiet so I had a peep and saw he was kissing her.

He had her little top hiked up and was feeling her tits. I was watching from over the back of a couch and couldn't see what else he was doing with her until she tensed and let out a little yelp.

Dirk resumed kissing the girl and talking into her open mouth while his arm was flexing and moving slightly. I could smell the young woman's arousal and it sounded like there were fingers inside of her, squelching a little as they went in and out and rubbed her little button. Or so I imagined as I hurried back to a pot boiling over.

Dirk was still there in the lounge playing with the girl until the runabout returned with Clark and his university friend. Leonie retreated into her bedroom again and I saw her lying with her eReader, probably enjoying one of the steamy romances she was telling me all about.

The three men running our search now decided to switch tactics and scour the seabed in quadrants rather than one large area. Within an hour they had their first quadrant mapped and one dive site identified.

They anchored and the three of them suited up and dived in. Leonie was still in her bedroom reading but I heard her laugh and squeal. I checked on her to find young Santos enjoying a feel of her tits and a bit of an awkward looking kiss.

I watched the boy have his fun and held eye contact with the young woman. Her legs were bent up a little and swayed together. The boy kissed his way down and sucked one of her tits. I looked from her legs to her eyes then back to her legs. She parted them for me. Her panties were gone and her cunt looked reddened and her inner folds were glistening wet.

Young Santos kept sucking from one nipple to the other whilst rubbing down over her belly and feeling into her.

Her eyes widened as he inserted. He immediately started fingering her, spearing that one middle digit in and out.

Leonie was sitting up but resting back on her hands. Her eyes returned to focus on me again. Young Santos pulled his finger out and pushed her leg to spread her more. She let him do that and kept her legs spread wide while he resumed fingering her. He was still sucking her tits, excitedly, noisily.

The radio was going off up in the bridge. The boy groaned anxiously and looked back at the doorway. "Aw shit, I've got to get that," he said to me. "Do you want her for a minute?"

He abandoned the young wife and rushed past me. Ooh yes indeedy did I want her, but I knew what she might be ready for too, so I approached and crawled onto the bed to lie across it on my back.

"Um..?" she questioned smilingly as I took her hand and tugged her over me.

She understood of course, and as she had done the last time, her demeanour instantly changed and she took hold of my hair and straddled my mouth and bearded face.

174

The girl was so wet and open. Her cunt had the distinct scent of sex – she had recently been fucked.

She squished herself open over my chin and rubbed her cunt upward until her swollen clit was pressed against my teeth, then she squished backward and ground against my whiskery chin again. She settled into a deliberate thrust and grind that had her cunt sliding back and forth and I growled into her opening and lashed with my tongue and bared my teeth when she forced her clit against them.

Her juices dripping and sometimes gushing into my mouth and all over my face were more musky and not entirely feminine. I wasn't going to protest and deny her for that. She was obviously for the taking by any of us men and it seemed someone had already fucked her, unless it had just been her husband.

"Uh huh huh," she moaned and tensed up, clenching her thighs against my shoulders and throwing her head back as her slender body convulsed. Her tits shuddered and wobbled up under her little crop top.

She tipped over and slumped beside me on the bed. "Mmm you bad man, that was so nice."

"Yeah I figured it was about your turn, love."

"Hmm yes, but this is all my turn. I love anything you men do with me. It doesn't matter if it's only you getting off or enjoying playing with my boobs or whatever, I still love it."

"Ah that's good. That's perfect love. I might need to pop one of my little blue pills and see what you're up to later then. Afternoon or evening is better for me."

The girl smiled back at me and shrugged a little. "Anytime you want, Linus. And you men are allowed to fuck me now. Clark and I talked. And Professor Norris already had me this morning."

"Ah I thought so. I thought you tasted different to last time."

"Mmm sorry. Obviously I can't help that though." The girl grimaced. "I hope that doesn't mean I have to miss out in future, does it?"

"No! Of course not love. Likewise – anytime you want to sit on my face like that. Absolutely anytime!"

"Hmm good." The girl kissed me quickly. "Because you've got the best face to sit on, if you didn't know already. I love how wiry and scratchy this is," she said, mussing my beard.

We shared a laugh but were interrupted by Professor Norris at the door. "Ah sorry, didn't mean to disturb."

"No that's fine, I have cooking to do, meals to prepare," I said and got up, leaving young Leonie with a squeeze of her hand.

I returned to chopping vegetables and sorting my kitchen. Soon enough I heard Leonie cry out, then there was the sound of her being pounded into the bed.

I took a tea towel, wiping my hands in it as I snuck and peeped in through the partially open bedroom door.

This new professor was nailing her. He was on top of her between her spread legs, thrusting powerfully and splitting her with a rather large looking penis. Her arms were flopped away from her body. The man was covering her and crushing her to him as he thumped into her, his balls slapping her arse. They were also quite oversized.

I watched fascinated, thinking that I would need to wait a few hours at least for her to have time to tighten up inside after this. She was being plunged so deep and no doubt her inner walls were being stretched and forced open. My unfortunate little member would scarcely touch the sides too soon after this absolute reaming the young wife was getting.

Leonie

I watched Linus watch me being fucked. I was trying to remain relaxed under Professor Norris but he was so huge and spearing into me so deep and nice. My orgasm was building and just about to overpower me when my husband appeared next to Linus and looked at me being fucked as well.

I bit down hard on my lip as the excitement of being taken like this and the amazing feel of Professor Norris's cock sent me over the edge. I lay completely still with my arms and legs resting open, but Professor Norris must have felt my orgasm because he stopped thrusting and remained still inside me.

"Oh yeah cum on me," he groaned into my hair, keeping my body crushed to his.

My pussy throbbed on his huge cock. I felt myself squeezing it with each contraction clenching my belly. He waited until my orgasm began to subside then he resumed fucking me.

I lay there completely limp for him, watching my husband and Linus. Professor Norris started thrusting faster and harder. He was rocking my legs wide open and I could hear his balls slapping against me. Then suddenly he powered hard into me and held firm. "Oh fuck yeah," he groaned into my ear and I felt his huge cock boned all the way up inside me. It began to throb and he let out another groan of pleasure.

I remained completely relaxed beneath the man and impaled on his shaft. I waited patiently while he emptied his big balls in me again. I wasn't sure if I could feel the spurts but I was imagining them and was so excited to be getting filled with more of his sperm like this. He's such a big strong man and it felt so right somehow.

"There you go Leonie, there's a top-up for you eh!"

"Uh huh thank you," I whispered back. "Thank you for fucking me again, Professor Norris."

179

He covered my mouth with his and kissed me deeply whilst moving inside me again. I noticed Linus was asking my husband something and Clark just nodded in answer, his arms folded and his jaw set.

Linus went back to his galley. Clark gave me a little wave and turned away too. The man on top of me was still semi-firm and continued fucking me whilst ravaging my mouth with his tongue. I lay there with legs and mouth open for him to enjoy.

"Okay I'd better get back to it. Until later, yeah? I might fuck you again tonight."

I swallowed and nodded a little. "If you want to. Before bedtime though please? I still want to sleep with my husband."

"Haha sure. As long as I get to top you up before you get into bed with him. Although I pump mine in a bit deeper," he teased into another kiss whilst feeling like he was flexing fully erect again.

"Uh huh it certainly feels deeper than Clark does inside me. I love it," I confessed to the guy. "I love being full of your sperm right now, Professor Norris. I hope I felt nice enough that you want to keep fucking me tonight and tomorrow and as long as you're here with us."

"Yeah this has got me thinking now, Leonie. I could take some leave. I don't see why I need to rush home if you're available to fuck like this. I could stay and help with the salvage if we can find this wreck."

I nodded and took a breath. "It would be fine by me. I'd love for you to stay and I'm definitely available for you to fuck." He pulled back and thrust again. "Uh huh huh I think that spot right there deep inside is all yours."

"Ooh yeah that's good. I'll talk to Clark then. Let him know I'll be staying on so I can keep fucking his wife deeper than he can himself." The man got up off me and pulled up his pants. "I'll tell him how much you like your belly full of my sperm, shall I?"

"Hmm fine. I'll tell him myself anyway," I shot back defiantly. "Since it's true!"

They were calling for Professor Norris upstairs. He rushed off and I used my discarded panties to dab my poor pussy dry. I put on my bikini bottoms and took off my crop top.

I went up onto the deck topless and did some sunbathing whilst all the men gawked or smiled at me. Linus loved playing waiter and without Victoria around I was getting all the attention. He served me lunch and started giving me fruity umbrella drink cocktails.

The men had identified another dive site. They dropped anchor and Clark and Professor Norris went down to see what this particular symmetrical formation was. It turned out to be an old wooden-hulled boat from about a century ago and they decided to salvage some artefacts from it. There were some interesting crockery pieces and a spear of some kind and an ancient gun.

Clark and the professor were busy diving and bringing things up to clean and check out. Dirk took my hand and led me down the stairs.

It had been a couple of hours since Professor Norris fucked me so I was feeling relaxed and mostly recovered down there. Dirk is pretty huge too but not as long as Professor Norris. He pulled off my bikini pants and went down on me, licking me wet and open. I lay there twirling my hair and watching him undress his t-shirt to reveal his chiselled torso and huge shoulders. When he pushed down his swim shorts his cock sprung horizontally and bounced, making me smile up from it.

"Hey baby, been thinking about this ever since we left home. You ready?" he asked as he lowered on top of me.

I didn't answer. I never do. I just lay there and stared back at the guy.

He chuckled and lifted one of my legs, fisted his cock and pressed the head against my pussy, then lay down on me and thrust.

I opened my mouth, silently squealing. He was actually quite thick and stretched me. I wasn't quite wet enough without the lube my husband usually applies before taking me cold like this.

Dirk must have read my mind or picked up on my discomfort. I'd left Clark's lube on the bedside table in case one of the men needed it. Dirk grabbed the bottle and squeezed some into his hand, lubricated his cock with it then repeated the process from before, this time stretching me so nice as he slid all the way in.

"Better?" he asked but I still didn't answer. He chuckled some more and held me by the top of the head whilst settling into rhythm fucking me for his pleasure. This time it was young Santos watching from the doorway. I lay there watching his excited face and enjoyed being taken in front of him.

"Nya fuck!" the man on top of me cried out and thumped hard against me to hold firm with his cock throbbing powerfully inside me.

I was completely relaxed on his cock, his balls resting against my butt. They were pulsating too. "That's it darlin', take it," Dirk breathed into my hair. "Ooh you're so fucking tight."

I remained silent, just biting my lip and keeping completely still for the guy as well, letting him inseminate me like the naughty girl piggy did with her three boar friends at that farm in New Zealand.

Dirk hadn't even kissed me but that was fine too. He finished cumming and got up off me, motioning for young Santos to come in. "Here, have a go kid. Come get some taboo married pussy. The best kind hey!"

I couldn't help blushing but remained silent and lay there submissively. The deck hand was holding his erection in his shorts. The yacht captain fixed his hair in my mirror whilst his helper pushed down his shorts and crawled between my legs up on top of me. He jiggled and probed my crotch. I had to reach down and guide him and when he poked a little way into my vagina he suddenly thrust and jammed himself hard against me.

Dirk stopped at the doorway and watched. I met his eyes and held them while the boy fucked me. He was squirming and humping uncontrollably, keeping himself jammed all the way up me and going off like a vibrating toy.

"Uh uh uh huh huh," he moaned raggedly then was suddenly still and clamped to me, his thin body flexed taut and quivering, his cock inside me throbbing away.

I looked to our yacht captain. He glanced from watching me being inseminated again. He winked. "That's good darlin'. There's a good wife."

I blushed deeper and held the younger man's hips, keeping my legs spread wide for him and wanting him to stay inside me and enjoy this.

"Come on then kid, that'll do you," his boss said though.

Santos got up off me and didn't look back on his way out the door. He left me needing to hold my pussy closed to stop from dripping everywhere. I was still quite open from Dirk and they both seemed to cum quite a lot.

"You okay baby?" my husband asked, suddenly there at the door.

I nodded, biting my lip and grimacing guiltily because of how much I was enjoying this. I had already been topless and now was completely naked. I stood a little shakily and grabbed a hand towel from the ensuite to hold over my pussy. "I'm okay, I'm just dripping," I explained to my husband. "They must have all been saving up. It feels like they're all cumming so much in me."

"Oh right. So that was Santos just now, and Dirk and Norris as well huh?"

"Uh huh." I cuddled close to my husband. He stroked my hair from my sweaty face and looked into my eyes but there was suddenly a shout from up on deck.

There was a commotion down the stairs and Santos was there at the bedroom door red-faced and excited. "You gotta come have a look boss. Professor Norris found something!"

Epilogue

Professor Norris had found a British artefact, a cigar box with an imprinted coat of arms. Clark joined in diving again and they tracked debris to another formation behind the old fishing boat they had been salvaging artefacts from. There they found the hull of the HMS Sunline. And just on dark they emerged with a chest that could have once held some kind of treasure but now was empty.

"Hell yes, I'm definitely sticking around for this," Professor Norris declared. "Damn it Clark, do you have any idea how huge a find this is?"

Linus confirmed too that he was up for financing the salvage mission and if more equipment was needed, where did he have to sign for it?

"Fuck yes I'm in," Dirk told everyone excitedly. "That's a fucking treasure chest!"

We ate up on deck. Linus put on one of his best barbeques and everyone got very merry and partied hard to celebrate the success of our adventure at sea.

Clark and I found a quiet spot to chat privately. It had been a whirlwind day in several ways.

"Okay so now the real adventure begins pulling up anything we can find from this wreck, baby, but how is it going with this other little adventure we're on? Are you still okay with being shared amongst these men like this?"

"Um yes, I'm still okay with it, Clark. I'm happy to play my part here."

"Okay good baby, but it's only because we're all the way out here in the middle of the ocean, right? There's no way we would want anything like this to happen back home."

"No I know," I agreed softly, peering up at my worried husband. "Professor Norris knows that too Clark. I love that he's already fucked me twice today and that he's going to again later tonight, but he knows it's only because we're out to sea and so far away from home."

"Oh hell, he's going to fuck you again tonight?" my husband asked anxiously.

"Um yes he is and I can hardly wait because of how deep he can penetrate me, Clark." I lifted to whisper close. "Dirk and Santos both flooded me with their cum but I seriously felt like Professor Norris was spurting directly into my belly."

"Ah shit."

"Mmm and all day it's felt like my womb is all warm and alive with his sperm." I took a shallow breath. "But that's just silly, right?'

"Oh hell baby, I don't know what it is. It's something!"

I was being pulled by the hand. It was Linus. I submitted to him and he led me downstairs to the cheers of everyone and a lingering angst-filled look from my husband.

Linus had indeed taken a blue pill. He was fully erect when he lowered his pants. I scooted back on the bed and lay facing away from him. I had an idea I wanted to try.

"Um can you use my husband's lube please?" I asked him, peering back over my shoulder.

He squeezed a liberal amount and covered his penis with it. "Like that?"

I nodded. "Now I'm going to be a ragdolly for you in a minute but I want you to try me from behind, okay?"

He got on the bed, lying behind me. "Like this?"

"Uh huh," I said, blushing fully and reaching between my legs to take hold of his slippery cock. "Mmm like that," I said to him and held the head against my anus as he thrust. His small but very hard cock popped into me and he immediately thrust and impaled me with it.

"Oh my, that's um…"

"Uh huh, do you like?"

He started fucking me, only pulling out a little way then thrusting back into me.

"Mmm you feel so naughty in me like that, Linus. I'm just going to relax and let you do whatever you want now okay."

I curled up with my hands beneath my chin and lay there while the older man fucked me. He was groaning and muttering about how tight I was and how he'd never tried this before in his whole life. I kept silent and completely relaxed for him. He soon got excited and worked me over onto my front. He straddled my butt and used his pelvis to hump me, gripping my shoulders and riding me until he suddenly lost it and speared all the way up to hold firm.

"Ah love," he groaned one last time and for the next little while the only part of either of our bodies moving was his cock pulsating inside me.

He slumped on my back and kissed my cheek. "Oh love that was amazing."

"Uh huh, I'm glad you liked it."

He was still inside me, still pumped up hard on his boner drug. He joked. "Ooh that was so satisfying. I think that was an exceptionally large ejaculate for me, love. I hope you like it inside you there."

191

"Uh huh I do like it. Thank you so much, Linus. Maybe you could do that to me sometimes if those other guys are going to be having turns in me the other way?" I asked hopefully.

*

Later that week, after being taken at will by all these virile men whenever they needed it, I noticed I was late for my period. Then after another week of being fucked from behind and in my mouth by Linus and my husband, and being rag-dolled and cummed inside by the yacht captain, Professor Norris, and the young deckhand, Clark and I took the water taxi to Tonga and got a home pregnancy test kit.

I emerged from our hotel bathroom and showed him the result we both expected.

He tugged me onto his lap, took a breath and expelled. "Well, it could still be mine, right?"

"Uh huh it could be…"

** The end **

Made in the USA
Monee, IL
07 December 2024

72832251R00108